THE LIFE AND TIMES OF EDWARD MORGAN

JOE SCIPIONE

D & T
PUBLISHING

For Isabella, who sat next to me while I wrote every single word of this story.

1

Edward Morgan put his hand on Jarvis's shoulder and thrust his blade into the First Mate's gut. Shouts of the men around them faded into the background as Jarvis's body tensed and then relaxed against him. Morgan leaned against Jarvis. The body slumped into him and Morgan let the man's body weight drive the blade further into his belly.

"Don't ever cheat me, Jarvis," Morgan whispered into Jarvis's ear. They both smelled of sweat. Morgan hated the fact that he was this close to the cheater, but took joy knowing his life was ending. Even when Morgan pulled the blade back only to thrust it in a second time, he knew there was going to be hell to pay when Captain Avery got word of what happened. In the moment, however, he didn't care. The consequences—whatever they turned out to be—would be worth it to feel the life drain out of the first mate.

Hands gripped Morgan's shoulders and he turned the knife inside Jarvis a few more times, first right as hard as he could then back left, working the point of the blade back and forth as he did, hoping to hit as many of the man's vital organs as he could before they pulled apart. Warm, sticky blood gushed out of Jarvis and coated Morgan's fist.

"Enough, enough," a voice said from behind Morgan. It was the first words he could make out since walking up to Jarvis and plunging the knife into his belly a few moments before. The stab wound was enough to kill him, Morgan made sure of it. Wiggling and twisting the knife inside of him took care of any chance Jarvis had of surviving the initial stab wound. Morgan wanted the cheater to suffer, but also wanted to be positive he died and wasn't saved by some miracle cure.

"Alright," Morgan said. He slid the knife back and forth inside Jarvis one final time before pushing the dying man away and yanking the blade out as quick and with as much force as he could muster. Jarvis collapsed to the wooden deck of the ship, gasping and holding his stomach. Morgan looked down at him and smiled as the blood seeped out through his fingers and soaked the wood of the ship.

Arms wrapped right around Morgan; this was the part he was dreading. He knew he'd have to face Captain Avery and suffer through the horrible things he had in store for him as a result of killing the first mate. But it was worth it.

"Cuff him up," Avery's gruff voice barked from somewhere behind Morgan. Morgan, doing his part, struggled against the men holding him, but there were too many and the crew was too fearful of Avery to disobey an order—even if they hated that cheating bilge-sucker Jarvis as much as Morgan did.

"What's his name?" Avery said to someone as iron cuffs were placed around his wrists and tightened in place.

"Name's Edward Morgan," Morgan said. He didn't need any other men to talk for him. He knew them all—only one or two were people he considered friends—he wasn't about to let them talk for him. Morgan was relatively new on the ship; this was his first cycle across the Atlantic and back. He was his own man, even Avery didn't scare him. Though what Avery might do to him for murdering his first mate did worry him.

Avery's worn, pock-marked, leathery face appeared in front of

Morgan, his grey beard stuck out in all directions. Avery stared at Morgan; his silver eyes bright with rage.

"The hell is the meaning of this, Morgan?" The Captain growled in his usual gravelly tone.

"I killed Jarvis, Captain. He's a facking cheat and stole m'money. To me that's enough for what he got. But he's cheated most men on the ship too. I guess I was just the one who stood up to 'em."

"Morgan," Avery smiled, his yellow teeth turning black at the gums. Morgan had never seen him smile and never wanted to see it again. "You killed the first mate and I should cleave you to the brisket for that. Regardless of how much money he cheated outta everyone on the ship. After I do that, I'd toss ya overboard and let the sharks gnaw on you for a while. I could just toss you off as you are, let them sharks eat you up alive. I'd love to hear the screams of a murderer getting eaten alive. But I got something even better in store for you. You think you're a tough man, do ya?"

The other men had backed away except one, who kept a tight grip on Morgan's collar to keep him from going after Avery. Morgan was pretty well shackled and didn't think he would be able to hurt the Captain, even if he had a mind to do so. Sweat dripped from Morgan's brow, his stomach churned. Avery was known for his ruthless tactics on the sea, Morgan's punishment might be worse than anything he could imagine.

"Aye," Morgan said. He nodded staring into Avery's rage filled eyes.

Avery stared back at him. For a moment, neither man moved, then Avery threw his head back and exploded with laughter. Around them, the others joined him. Morgan looked around, even the men he knew well were laughing. No one wanted to incur the wrath of Captain Avery. As long as there was a target for his rage and violence, the others were happy to keep their names out of his mouth. Morgan understood that, but he'd also remember the name of every man who was laughing at him. If he had the chance, he'd kill them all.

The laughing continued—the uproar cut through the silence of the vast empty ocean around them. Their bellows rose through the hot, humid air and reach the sun, which beat down on them incessantly day after day.

Then Avery's laughing stopped. A thud buried itself in Morgan's gut. Avery had punched him. The surrounding laughter ceased.

"Strip his shirt," Avery barked. The men followed his order, tearing the fabric of Morgan's shirt at the collar.

"Push his head down," Avery gave a second order, again the men obeyed instantly. Morgan tried to push back against them. He didn't know what Avery was going to do and didn't want to find out. He'd rather just be thrown over the side. From his bowed position, Morgan could see Avery's belt and his feet, but not much else. Out of the corner of his eyes there was movement and the unmistakable sound of a knife being pulled from its sheath. "Hold him still."

The grip on Morgan tightened. There must have been five or six men leaning on him because he couldn't move in any direction. White hot pain burned into Morgan's back. He gritted his teeth; he wasn't going to let Avery—or anyone else—have the satisfaction of hearing him scream. The men cheered, Avery started laughing again as the knife dragged through the meat of his back. The pain worsened. Morgan worried he'd pass out before this was done. Was this how he would die? He knew nothing. His breathing quickened, and the world began to spin. The pain was too much; it wouldn't be long now. Blood dripped around his chest and down onto the deck below, rippling in the pools of Jarvis's blood.

"That's enough for now," Avery grumbled, and the Captain's shoes disappeared. "Bring him to the brig."

Morgan's eyes fluttered closed and his legs gave way. The deck of the ship, soaked in both his and Jarvis's blood, rushed toward him. Then everything went black.

2

Morgan awoke in the brig unsure of how much time had passed. The lacerations crisscrossing his back were leaking blood and pus. It didn't take long for him to figure out that it was more comfortable to lay on his stomach, even with his wrists in cuffs and trapped underneath him. Apparently, after Avery sliced up his back, there had been no further repercussions or punishments. Even though the cuts hurt, Morgan could tell they were shallow. While there was always a risk for infection with an open wound on the sea, he knew the surface abrasions put him at minimal risk.

What worried Morgan the most, however, was the fact the Avery had never gone easy on anyone in his life, at least if the legends about the Captain were to be believed. Morgan had seen enough of Captain Avery in the few months he'd been aboard the *Glory* to understand that the rumors were true. Avery was ruthless and had a penchant for violence. That fact scared Morgan the most. He'd murdered the first mate—Avery's right-hand man—so the lack of punishment meant something more was coming. Morgan had a feeling it would be something terrible.

There was a metallic clang from somewhere in the darkness outside of the cage in the belly of the ship. Morgan squinted into the darkness and saw nothing at first. Then a faint light appeared from somewhere outside his field of vision. The light grew, and a candle appeared.

"Edward," the familiar voice said from beyond the candle's light. "Edward, you awake yet?"

"I am. Is that you, Peter?" Morgan replied. Peter Cooke was the closest thing Morgan had to a friend on the ship.

"Aye. Brought you a helping of food, I did. Captain's orders. He doesn't know we're friends though; I gather. But he's been having me check on you." Peter pushed a small bowl through the bars of the cell. "Small piece of beef and some beans is all, but it's as much as they would give me."

"Thank you," Morgan said. He was facedown and dragged himself across the floor, not bothering to lift his head up as dirt and damp wood dragged across his cheek. pushed himself across the floor on his face, using his knees and feet to slide forward. He wasn't able to get his hands up to grab the food, so he pushed his face against the bowl and grabbed at the dried meat with his lips. He chewed and gnawed at it until it was soft enough to swallow. "You know this is bad for me, Peter."

There was silence from outside the cage.

"You know it, even if you can't say it," Morgan continued. "He must have something terrible in mind for me if he's sending food down. Must have something he needs to keep me alive for."

"Can't think that way, Edward." The candle moved back and forth with the motion of the ship. Morgan couldn't see Peter's face in the darkness. As much as Morgan put up a hard exterior, it was good having at least one person he could count on.

"I'm not the kind of person to hope for the best, Peter. Anything else he needs you to do for me?"

"No."

"Then leave. Last thing you want is Avery to realize you're talking to me. Best if you keep your distance, too. I'm dead anyway."

The candle remained for a moment, though Morgan couldn't see

Peter's face, he could sense the worry. Then the candle vanished, and the brig returned to the unyielding, total darkness.

Morgan didn't move. He stayed like that—his face pressed against the floor, hands trapped beneath him—and prayed for death. If death came looking for him in the cell instead of in the face of whatever Avery had in mind for him, he would welcome it. A quiet death in the belly of the *Glory* was better than a bloody painful one at the mercy of Avery's warped imagination. Death didn't come for him. Exhaustion, however, did. Within minutes—the meager meal still digesting in his stomach—Edward Morgan fell asleep.

3

When he woke, the candle was back on the other side of the iron bars, but Peter's voice didn't accompany the dim light this time.

"Most times, you'd be dead already, you know that, Mr. Morgan?" Avery's voice was not the usual barking Morgan had heard on deck. The Captain's voice was still rough, as if there was a constant collection of phlegm somewhere in the back of his throat, but he was quieter than usual. Maybe, Morgan hoped, Avery hated Jarvis and no one knew about it. Maybe the Captain was happy about his death. It was the only hope Morgan had left.

"I know. Why am I not dead then?" Morgan rolled onto his side, laying on the floor looking up at the space just above the flame where he imagined Avery's face would be.

Avery laughed, "could be lots of reasons. Why do you think?"

"I don't know," Morgan groaned, trying to sit up, but the cuts on his back twisted when he moved and pulled open just enough to send a wave of pain through him. He grimaced and returned to his horizontal position. "You secretly hated Jarvis? Maybe he cheated you, too."

Avery laughed again; his deep chortle echoed in the small room. "You got a lot to learn about this business, Morgan. You want to be successful pirating like this, you either learn quick or die."

Avery's talk of Morgan learning fast gave him hope; maybe he'd get a second chance after all.

"Jarvis was a cheat," Avery went on. "Cheated everyone on the ship, gambling for as long as I can remember. He'd been with me coming on twenty years now."

"I believe it." Morgan said, his hope rising once again.

"But in twenty years, ain't never seen anyone dumb enough to accuse the first mate of cheating, Mr. Morgan. That is, until you were stupid enough to kill the poor bastard."

"So, you're going to let me go?" Morgan didn't care for the Captain's story time and just wanted to know what the final result would be.

Avery laughed again. Morgan sighed.

"Of course not. I'm Captain Avery. I kill crew for *fun,* Morgan, and you murdered my first mate. A deed like that can't go unpunished."

"So—" Morgan started but the intimidating Captain interrupted.

"Let me finish, there." Avery shouted and stood, slamming his hand against the iron bars. It made Morgan jump. "It can't go unpunished. You haven't been here long so let me fill you in. The other men, they know this story, maybe not so much for you. There's an old pirate tale about an island not far from here. Some think it's a myth, lad. Some don't. Men on my ship know it's there because we've been there, many a-time. It's called Dead Man's Isle. There's no food there. Even fish avoid the shores. No fresh water because it never rains. Among pirates, we consider it a death sentence if you get left there."

"You're bringing me there, I take it?"

"Aye, but there's more. It's a death sentence to be left there, but not everyone who has been left there has died. Some survive and when they do, their punishment has been served. That could be you Mr. Morgan."

"How do you know someone has made it off alive? Sounds like more myth to me."

"Aye, because I was about your age when my Captain dropped me off there. I killed three men aboard his ship. They disrespected me. I didn't care that it was my first year on a ship. I demanded respect. I explained to the Captain—same way you explained your problem with Jarvis. You, Edward, remind me a lot of myself. Your disloyalty must be punished. That's what the Captain said to me before he left me there, and that's what I'll say to you now. If you survive, the punishment will be served and you will come aboard again a new man. You'll have the respect of every member of this ship as well, including her Captain."

"Why help me? Because I remind you of yourself?" Morgan couldn't stop himself. He'd been granted a reprieve, of sorts. All he had to do was survive the island.

"Because there are men built for life on the sea and there are men built to *rule* the sea. I think you're meant to rule the sea, Mr. Morgan. You just have to prove it to me."

Morgan tried to push himself up. His back didn't hurt as much anymore. He felt invigorated. Not long ago, the challenge of the sea lay before him. Now there was a new challenge in front of him.

"You survived there?" Morgan grunted as he spoke, feeling the pus and blood drip down his back. His skin stretched and the movement caused the scabbing wounds to open up once more.

"Aye, it is a terrible place. But survive and the world opens up for you. No one will trifle with a man who survived Dead Man's Isle. But beware Morgan," Avery pulled up his shirt, his stomach and chest were a maze of scars. "The isle changes a man. My back has twice as many and my legs are just as bad."

Avery's chest and stomach were a map that told a story. Morgan didn't want to know the story, but realized if he was going to live, he'd learn parts of Avery's story and end up writing a new chapter in the lore of Dead Man's Isle.

"We will be there in just under two days. I'll keep sending your friend in with food and water. Eat up and stay strong, Mr. Morgan.

You will need it. We will be back in twenty days or so. It's a long time, but if you survive, you'll become a legend. We could take the seas together after that. No one could slow us down."

"Aye, I'll do my best." Morgan sat up as straight as he could.

"You need more than your best to survive the Isle. You'll need your worst too. That's all I'll tell ya lad. The rest is up to you."

Avery puffed out the candle, and the room was sent back into darkness. The heavy door opened and closed, and Morgan was alone once again. He let out a long slow breath and forced himself to his feet. In a few days, he was going to begin a fight for his life. He'd need to save up his strength, but he'd also need to be able to stand, move around, and figure out how he was going to stay alive for twenty days without food and water.

4

The next few days passed quickly. Avery did not visit again. The Captain had a ship to run and Morgan was a criminal, it didn't matter that Avery wanted Morgan to come back to the ship alive. Peter was allowed to bring Morgan food and fresh water three times a day, which would have been unheard of for most prisoners in the brig. It told Morgan that Avery was not just telling him what he wanted to hear, but he was backing up his words with actions. It didn't matter how feared and reviled the Captain was, he'd treated Morgan fairly, and thus was a good man in Morgan's estimation.

It was hard to determine the speed of the boat from inside the hull, but Morgan could tell by the way the *Glory* rocked slowly back and forth that their forward motion had slowed or possibly stopped.

"Edward," Peter's voice called from somewhere beyond the door to the brig. Morgan hadn't filled Peter in about what Avery had told him. As far as Morgan knew, no one on the ship knew where they were headed or for what purpose. Morgan focused all his mental and physical energy on what lay ahead for him.

"Edward," Peter repeated himself when he pushed the door open and entered. "We've stopped near an island. The rumor is its Dead

Man's Isle. The Captain wants you above deck. I don't know what he's planning."

Morgan stood, the bones in his knees and back cracked and popped as he rose. His back had healed a little, but it was still hard to move. The scabs and cuts remaining still hurt. Over the course of the next twenty days he was on the isle, they might heal completely. Assuming he survived.

Peter led him through the ship, up the narrow stairway to the top deck. The sun was bright and Morgan had been alone in mostly dark for four or five days at his estimation. The bright sun made him squint; he brought his cuffed hands up to his face to block the light. Eventually, his eyes adjusted. He blinked a few times and was able to see normally.

A large contingent of the crew met him on deck. Their cold stares bore a hole through Morgan, he ignored them. This was his challenge. There was a narrow path through the men, Morgan stood on one end and Captain Avery waited for him at the other. Some of the men might know they are at Dead Man's Isle, but Morgan didn't know how many of them had been here before and how many of them were making their first trip, same as him. For that reason, he kept the amount of information he knew about what was happening to himself.

"Make way for the prisoner," Avery barked in the gruff tone that was uniquely his. The narrow path through the men widened. Peter was in front of Morgan, but he moved to the side and joined the throng of men. Morgan stepped forward, his gaze at the wooden deck, not making eye contact with any of the men or with Avery.

When he reached Avery, Morgan took his first glance off the ship. The Isle was close, but it looked like his punishment was going to start with a swim. From where the ship had anchored, he could see the Isle was small. There was sand, and off to one side a small rocky area. A few plants stuck up from somewhere not too far inland, as well as two good sized trees. But other than that, it looked barren, empty.

Avery snatched Morgan's hands and jerked him forward, then

unlocked the cuffs, releasing him for the first time since the day he killed Jarvis.

"The prisoner, Edward Morgan, is accused of murdering Mr. Jarvis in cold blood. There were several witnesses. Do you agree with the accusation, Mr. Morgan?"

"I agree."

A murmur passed through the throng of men behind him. Morgan didn't know what they expected. Maybe they wanted him to fight the Captain, or they were hoping Avery would take a blade to him and end it right then. But it didn't happen.

"Then your sentence shall be death through pain and suffering on the island known as Dead Man's Isle."

The men spoke amongst themselves louder than before. Morgan was probably the only one aboard who knew next to nothing about the isle. He was glad he didn't know the myths because he was certain the myths made the place seem worse than it actually was. None of the men, he guessed, knew Captain Avery was a survivor of the place.

"Edward Morgan will be removed forcefully from the *Glory* and he will swim to the isle. We will then raise anchor and leave. In twenty days, or there about, we will return to inspect the remains of Mr. Morgan. This shall be his punishment for the murder of the first mate Mr. William Jarvis."

More whoops and hollers from the men. Morgan gritted his teeth.

Avery took a step toward Morgan and grabbed him hard by the shoulders. The Captain took Morgan's wrist and twisted it behind his back. Holding the opposite shoulder, he steered Morgan to the side of the ship.

"The isle might have some surprises for you. Good luck, kid." Avery whispered in his ear. Then he pushed Morgan to the side of the ship, leaned all his weight against him, and released him. Morgan went tumbling head over heels into the churning water below. His face hit the surface of the water hard from the pinwheeling he did on the way down. Pressure built up in his ears and they rang as he went below the surface. His feet flailed as he attempted to right himself and determine which way to swim up to the surface. The salt water stung his back and eyes when he opened them to get his bearings. The sun shone through the clear blue water, giving Morgan a direction to swim toward. He kicked once, twice, a third time, and his face breeched the surface. He gave a look up at the ship above him; Avery, leaning over the side of the ship looking down at him, one side of his mouth turned up into a smile, that looked more like a sneer.

"Twenty days," Avery mouthed to him before turning and shouting something to the rest of the crew. Morgan turned and swam to shore.

By the time Morgan got close enough to the shore of the tiny isle for his feet to touch, his back was on fire. The salt water soaked his shirt and lay against the wounds that were nowhere near healed. He groaned as he walked on the sand, the water slowly receding from his chest, down to his waist, then his knees until he was standing on dry ground. His first order of business was to pull off his saltwater-soaked clothes that were doing nothing but making the pain worse.

Once his shirt was off and laying on a rock to dry, Morgan turned, gave a look to the tiny island—of which he could see almost two-thirds of just from where he was standing. Then he looked out to sea, at the *Glory* which was making its way toward whichever stop Captain Avery had in mind next. The ship wasn't Morgan's concern. His only task now that he made it to Dead Man's Isle, was his own survival.

5

His back stung, but he'd have to get used to it if he was going to survive the next few weeks. Morgan hadn't asked Avery for any advice surviving the isle, Avery wasn't exactly the kind of person who would give advice even if Morgan had asked for it. Help wasn't a word on the tip of Avery's tongue.

There were only about ten steps from the water's edge across the dry sand to the tall grass that grew thick at the middle of the isle. A few medium-sized palm trees stood over a small crest at the center of the isle. Small plants and bushes littered the isle, some of them bigger than they seemed from the deck of the ship. Morgan wanted to get an idea of just how small the isle was and wanted to know as much about it as he could. Since the isle was small enough, he decided a full tour of the whole place should be his first task. He shook out his shirt and put it back on. It was still damp and the salt water sting burned his cuts, but he gritted his teeth and pushed forward.

To his left there was a small rock cliff. If necessary, he could scale it as it was not much taller than he was, but Morgan didn't want to exert the effort if he didn't have to. However, knowing the layout of the isle was worth the energy.

Morgan approached the green area and put the water on his right. The *Glory* was small out on the horizon and getting smaller. He was on his own.

He followed the grass-sand line as he traversed the isle. So far, Avery had been correct, there was no food or fresh water on the isle. Everything was dry, the grass and trees meant it must rain some time or there was an underground water source. Morgan expected the rain fell mostly in the winter season, which was still months away. The height of the sun told him it was about two hours by the time he'd circled the entire isle, arriving back at the top of the rock ledge.

For the most part, the isle he saw while circumnavigating it was the same one he saw standing on the small beach. It was the same one he saw from the deck of the *Glory*. There was sand, grass, a few trees and bushes, some rocky areas, and that was it. He hadn't explored all of the green, inland area of the isle, but he didn't see anything that made him think the interior was much different than the rest of it, unless there were any small animals there to hunt. He could walk shore to shore, through the copse of palm trees and brush, in less than an hour, how much could be hidden in there?

Other than the fact that there didn't appear to be any food or water, the isle didn't seem as bad as Avery made it out to be.

Morgan returned to the beach where he first set foot on the Isle and decided to make it his home for the next few weeks until Avery and the *Glory* returned. He knew he was in for the fight of his life, but he also didn't see any reason why he wouldn't survive the ordeal. He could fish or eat enough of the plants, at least enough to survive the few weeks. Maybe it wasn't as bad as the myth—or Avery—made it out to be.

Morgan was a hothead; he'd been one his entire life. He'd been called out for his temper since he was a kid. the fact that he'd killed someone less than a year at sea would surprise no one who knew him. Least of all his mother, who was glad to be rid of him. After dealing with his temper for as long as she had. His father had the same temper and, when he was at home—which was not very much

—he took it out on his mother. Morgan saw the violent streak his father had and assumed it was where he got his own proclivity for violence. But he always promised himself he'd be different than his father. He could be violent, but there was always going to be a reason for it. It was never going to be violence for the sake of violence. His parents tried to give him a proper education, so they sent him to school. Morgan was smart. Very smart. But school and learning in books was not the way for Edward Morgan. Unsatisfied with that life, he decided to take to the sea. Once aboard a legitimate vessel, it wasn't long before Morgan encountered the pirate vessel *Glory*. Legitimate shipping didn't hold his attention after that. When he found himself in the same port as the *Glory*, he deserted his post and joined Avery's crew.

Morgan didn't take to the pirate life as quick as he thought he would—once again the temper was too much. He made a single friend in Peter, but he didn't bother getting to know the rest of the men very well. Most of the men had spent years aboard the *Glory* or other privateering vessels. They knew what they were doing and didn't want to show Morgan the proper way of doing things. Morgan resented them for this. If they gave him a hard time, he took it personally. He didn't want to stay on the *Glory* much longer, but wanted to make as much money as possible. He turned to gambling as a way to make more money while aboard the ship. He was good at gambling, but the men loved to cheat and they especially liked to cheat the new guy. If there was one thing Morgan couldn't stand, it was a cheat.

His temper had gotten him in trouble his whole life. Why did he think this would be any different? The good news, at least Morgan considered it good news, was when his temper got him in trouble, his smarts always got him out of trouble. On Dead Man's Isle, he was set up to have his smart wriggle him out of another jam.

The day was ending. Morgan hadn't seen or heard any animals, which would make sense so far from land of any type. His first thought was to make a fire, but that would require trudging into the grasses to find something to burn, and he figured staying on the sand and waiting until morning to make a fire and find some food and water made more sense.

Compared to the hard floor of the brig, the soft sand was going to be a great place to sleep. Morgan sat on the beach as the sun set, exhaustion hit him all at once and before he knew it, he was asleep.

6

It was still dark when a noise woke Morgan. His eyes opened, but he did not move. At first, Morgan imagined he was still in the brig and it took him a moment to remember he was alone on the beach at Dead Man's Isle. That memory was almost enough to set his mind at ease and put him back to sleep. Then the noise returned and Morgan was fully awake, listening and ready to react if necessary.

He mentally made a list of things that could have made the strange rustling sound. First, he assumed it was a light breeze moving the air in just the right way to shake a leaf or a few blades of tall grass. The air, however, was motionless. It could have been an insect or a turtle coming out of the water, but he doubted both of those possibilities. Luckily, the moon and the stars provided him with more light than he'd had in the brig, so he was could see the area around him with some clarity.

Morgan sat up. He scanned his immediate surroundings. There was only sand and rocks.

The horizon was black, there was no line separating the sky from ocean—still a lot of night left. Morgan drew his feet up and rested his elbows on his knees. He scanned the area once more and held his breath, listening for the sound again and looking for signs of movement. There was nothing.

Best to just lie back down and get more rest. Morgan straightened his legs out and moved to lay back on the soft sand when the rustling returned.

The noise was closer this time, and Morgan sat up once more and looked around. At first there was still nothing to see, but as he turned his head to the right, he caught movement Something faded into the darkness and it was big.

Morgan scrambled to his feet and moved, with an abundance of caution, toward the area he'd seen the movement. It was much bigger than a turtle and the way it had looked—in the fraction of a second Morgan had seen it—almost like another, bigger, human.

It was possible another ship had dropped someone off at Dead Man's Isle—maybe even after Morgan had fallen asleep. If they approached from the opposite side of the island, Morgan might never have seen them. Somehow, though, he didn't think it was the case. It was more likely the person was on the isle when Morgan arrived.

Morgan marched toward the last place he saw movement, but after a few steps into the dark interior of the isle, he realized he couldn't see anything hidden in the tall grass. A search of the isle was a task better suited for morning when there was light and more to see.

Morgan returned to his sleeping area, he gave passing thought to laying back down and trying to fall asleep, then decided against it. If someone else was on the isle with him, that person had snuck up on him while he slept. The 'other' knew more about Morgan than Morgan knew about them. He didn't like walking in blind to a situation like that. He'd wait until morning and scour the isle until he found whoever, or whatever was roaming in the darkness.

Sleep was going to be impossible to come by, so Morgan went to the rocky ledge and sat with his back against it. Nothing could come at him from behind, unless it wanted to drop down from the top of the ledge. Still, it would give Morgan an advantage. He kept his eyes open and watched darkness while he waited for morning.

Eventually, morning came, Morgan was tired, and there was another issue which had become pressing overnight. His stomach had begun to grumble and his mouth was starting to go dry. Not only was he not alone on the isle, but the effects of lack of food and water were already starting to rear their heads.

The horizon to his right turned a light shade of blue, then orange, before the bright yellow sun forced its way up from below clear water. Even in the midst of his supposed death sentence, Morgan could comprehend beauty in the sight. It was something he could see a thousand times and never tire of. The fact was not lost on him that if he didn't find a source of food and water soon, his sunrises were numbered.

When it was light enough out for him to see the ground clearly, Morgan stood up and stretched his legs. He hadn't moved from his seated position against the rock all night. The cuts on his back hurt, but the itching told him they were also continuing to heal.

He made a mental list of his top three priorities. The visitor from last night, water, and food. While he knew the visitor should have been third on the priority list, his curiosity was going to get the better of him. Without much thought put in to where to find water or food, Morgan clenched his fists and pushed his hair back away from his eyes. He stared into the green inland of the isle and set off to find whatever it was that had come for him during the night.

Like the rest of the isle, the copse was not very large, Morgan figured he could be done searching before the sun reached its zenith leaving him the afternoon to determine a way to get food and water before he died of starvation or dehydration. Searching the middle of the isle was not a complete waste, but Morgan knew there were plants he could break in half and get some moisture from. If he saw large plants or anything that looked particularly ripe with fluids, he'd break it open and see what would come of it. His time without water was running thin. The plants were green—they were getting water from somewhere—he just had to find it.

The grass was about knee high, and Morgan walked through it, scanning his surroundings with each step. If it was a person who visited him last night, he needed to be ready for anything. They could have just been checking him out, eventually deciding to stay away, or they could be hiding—waiting for the right time to attack. If they were going to attack, Morgan was confident, but he had to be ready for anything.

He walked in a spiral pattern working his way around the island moving closer to the center. He'd repeat the process on the way out, but covering a different area. He wouldn't step on every piece of land on the isle, but he'd see it all. Ahead, almost at the exact center of the island, stood the pair of tall palm trees he'd seen for the first time on the *Glory*.

He affixed his gaze to the small space between the two trees. *That* was his destination. He'd end his search there, then walk in a similar spiral pattern out to the beach. By then he'd know the flat grassy isle as well as he was ever going to. He'd have seen the whole thing and would know what was on it, and what wasn't. Captain Avery's voice echoed in his head *"there is no food, no fresh water...the isle might have some surprises for you"* When Avery told him about the sentence, Morgan took it as a kind of reprieve, after having seen almost all of the isle, he realized how hopeless his situation might be.

The trees drew closer, he'd seen no sign of his visitor—also no signs of food or water. All he'd seen was the knee-high grass and a few small bushes, most of the leaves long since dried up and holding no berries.

The nearest palm tree stood a few paces in front of Morgan. It was taller than it looked from the water. He approached, staring up at the smooth trunk and the large flat leaves atop. He crouched down and peered between the leaves for coconuts, but there weren't any.

Finally, he stood between the two trees, still looking up, and checked the second tree for coconuts just in case. Distracted by the possibility of food above him, he didn't notice the large hole in the ground until he almost stepped in.

"Jesus," Morgan said under his breath. He jumped back, then approached the hole with more caution. The grass was long enough and hung in such a way that the opening to the hole was almost completely disguised. Even knowing it was there, it looked more like a patch of dark soil than an opening in the earth. But that was exactly what it was. Morgan used his foot to pull back some of the grass and then reached down and grabbed at it, ripping it out so the sun—which was almost directly overhead—could shine down into it. He thought it was a hole leading straight down into the earth, but it wasn't just a hole, it was a cave. There were a few steps down and then the rocky floor of the cave smoothed out. It descended at a sharp angle and disappeared under the isle. At least now, Morgan knew where his visitor had come from and where they were hiding.

He gave a look up to the sun. If there was someone else living here on the isle, then they had food and water. If it was someone dropped there as punishment, like Morgan had been, then they could work together to survive the isle. He hoped it was a person or people living on the isle because it would mean a source of food and water. If they had it, Morgan needed to get some of it, so he changed his plans. Everything he was looking for could be in the cave, so he put one foot, then the other onto the first rocky, jagged step. He moved down to the next one, took a few steps and then ducked his head, disappearing underneath Dead Man's Isle.

7

There was no light source inside the cave, the only reason he could see anything was the sunlight pouring in the hole from behind him. Morgan knew the light wouldn't last much longer.

He ran a hand along the wall, the stone was rough in some places, worn smooth in others. It was evident that this cave had been used before. Morgan could picture a person—maybe more than one person—walking up the cave toward the surface of the isle. Whoever it was would put a hand against the rock—always in the same place—then walking a few steps and putting their hand against the rock again. Over time, this would lead to the alternating worn and rough areas he discovered. But there were no other signs of life inside the cave. No tools littered the floor, no ashes from torches sprinkled along the rock, at least none Morgan could see. But *something* had to be down there. He had to keep going and see what was inside this cave.

He walked a few more steps, the light waned. It wouldn't be long before the cave was as dark as the brig aboard the *Glory*. If he spent enough time in the cave, his eyes would begin to adjust and he'd be able to see something.

Nothing but blackness in front of him, Morgan pressed on,

moving deeper down the slope which became steeper as he progressed.

Morgan sucked in a long deep breath and caught the odor of something he wasn't expecting. Burning wood.

The cavern was too dark for him to see smoke, if there was a lot, he would have seen it from the surface. The fact that he couldn't see it, didn't mean it wasn't there, it's just not visible. The scent was unmistakable. If there was burning wood, it could only mean one thing: other people.

Morgan kept going He felt himself pick up the pace because other people didn't just mean fire; it meant food, water, survival and a ticket off the isle when the *Glory* returned. When voices echoed up the narrow cave, Morgan slowed. He couldn't just walk in on the person, or people, living down below Dead Man's Isle. He needed to determine what he was going to do when he found them before he got there. There were, of course, two basic choices. He could be friendly with them, and get them to help. Or he could be violent, take their food and their water and survive on his own for the rest of the twenty days.

Violence—and his temper—was what got him stuck on the isle in the first place. Maybe he needed to try a different approach. He slowed his pace. At first, he continued his walk into darkness. Morgan kept a hand out in front of him as he went down the steep decline in case a rock jutted out from the walls of the cave or hung down from overhead. But then he saw a faint red light appear from below. It was the fire. However, much wood was burning down there, it was enough for Morgan to see it. He kept his eyes focused on the glowing red spot ahead of him as he walked, slowly and carefully, so as not to make any noise on his approach.

As Morgan drew closer, the voices got louder. But he realized he didn't understand the language. It wasn't French or Spanish or even German or Italian; all of which Morgan could recognize. No, this was a language he'd never heard before.

He came to the end of the narrow cave and there was a corner, the cave ended at a large open area. It was much brighter now.

Morgan leaned his back against the cool stone of the cave and peered around the corner. At the far end of a wide-open space was a small fire and two figures were seated around it. It was too far to make out what they looked like, just that they were there and apparently having a conversation.

Morgan watched for a moment, but in the very low light and at such a great distance, it was impossible to gather any more information about them. He'd have to get closer.

Stay calm, he told himself. Violence was not going to help him in this situation.

He turned the corner, took a few steps toward them and decided to call out to them, not loud, as sound would travel easily surrounded by stone. He decided to keep his voice low, almost quiet, so he wouldn't scare them.

"Hello," he said, assuming the people would know that word because it was similar in many languages.

Sudden movement. They turned toward him. It was still hard for him to see, but both figures looked in his direction. The figure closest to him said something low and quiet that Morgan couldn't hear. The figure that was further away appeared to rise to their feet. The second figure was dark, Morgan could just make out the shape of it, but it rose to its feet. Only then did Morgan realize how tall it was. The closer figure was not too far away, but the dark figure was massive, at least double Morgan's height from what he could tell. The dark figure then scampered off into the darkness, the echoing sound as it left the open area was not of footfalls against rock, but something different. Morgan didn't know what he was hearing.

The closer figure remained, and Morgan had to turn his attention to them. He still needed food and water.

Morgan advanced once more. He was cautious. He took a few steps and waited, when the figure didn't move, he took a few more. As he did so, he kept his hands out, palms facing forward to let the person know he wasn't a threat. It seemed to work because the person didn't move, and as Morgan got closer, he realized it was a girl—or woman—it was hard to tell because from what he could see, she was incredibly thin and emaciated, making it hard to place her age.

"My name is Edward," he said. His voice still soft, soothing. He could be good at the caring thing when he really worked at it. "Can you understand me?"

He could see her face now, weathered and wrinkled, dark with dirt and too much sun. She was at least as old as Morgan, if not older, but living in a cave on a deserted isle couldn't have been good for her health or her appearance.

She remained silent, but didn't look scared. Morgan gave a quick look off into the darkness where the large figure had disappeared.

"Do you understand me? I heard you speaking a different language." Morgan said again and waited. If she didn't answer this time, he would have to change his approach.

"Yes," she said. Her voice was weak and gravelly. As if a long hard life on an isle such as this changed your voice over time. "I know English."

"That's great. My ship sank not far from here. I was the only one who managed to survive, I think. I just happened to bump into this small island. I was hoping to find food or water. I didn't know someone else would be here."

"Yes, I am here. I have been here a long time." She sat back down where she'd been sitting before Morgan had called out.

"The two of you?" Morgan asked, his curiosity got the best of him.

The woman glanced off to her right where the other figure had run off and for the first time Morgan saw an expression on her worn face. It was only for a moment, but he was certain he saw the right side of her mouth curl up in a half smile. Whoever the other person was, the woman liked him. Maybe it was her husband, a lover, a child?

"Yes. Well, he has been here a lot longer than me," she said. Again, the half-smile grew on her face as she spoke.

"I understand," Morgan said, even though he didn't. "I scoured the island and didn't find any food or water. Do you have any I could borrow? I'm not sure how long I will be here, but I will need some food to eat."

The woman nodded and relaxed a bit in her seat. She motioned for Morgan to sit on the other side of the fire with her, but didn't say anything. Morgan's stomach rumbled, at the mere thought of food, his body responded.

"Food is hard to come by," she said. Her tone harder, she speech faster.

"What do you eat?"

"Usually, they drop 'em off and we catch them on the beach—the one you slept on last night. Never had anyone come right to us though," she looked at Morgan and smiled. Her teeth were yellow and brown, she'd lost a few of them already and more were sure to follow.

"What do you mean?"

"You'll understand," the woman stared at Morgan, held his gaze for just a moment, but it was just long enough for a pair of strong arms to wrap themselves around Morgan's chest. Something hit him in the back of the head and everything went black.

8

Cold wetness woke him. He screamed, blinked a few times and saw the woman standing over him, an empty bucket hanging from one hand. The world came into focus. He was still in the cave some-where, the dim glowing reddish-yellow light of fire danced across rock walls.

Morgan tried to move his arms and legs, he was tied, his arms were behind his back and his legs strapped together by some kind of rope, he couldn't get a good look.

"What are you doing?" He said to her. The calm, easygoing tone gone from his voice.

"You asked about food, didn't you?" She said it matter of fact, as if Morgan should have known what food had to do with him being knocked unconscious and tied up. "This is how we get our food."

"Who else is here? I don't see anyone."

The woman made a sound like something Morgan had never heard before. It was a phlegm-filled noise emanating from the back of her throat. She looked—and sounded—as if she was gagging. But then continued on as if there was no problem.

"...likes to make sure everyone he doesn't know is secure," she said.

"I'm sorry. Who does that?" Morgan felt as though he was drunk, nothing the woman said made any sense to him. He licked his lips and realized his mouth was incredibly dry, even after the bucket of water she dumped on him. He had no way of knowing how long he had been unconscious. When he'd gone down into the cave, it had already been a day without water, if he'd been out a while, he was getting dangerously close to dehydration.

The woman looked at him, tilted her head and made the phlegmy sound once again. "That's his name. The one you saw. The one who attacked you, that's his name."

"The tall one. Who is he? Why doesn't he want me to see him?"

"My lover," she said with a bat of her eyes and that half-mouthed smile she'd shown him earlier. "he's not like us though, not like you an' me. He's different, but I still love him."

"His name is in his language, then? He does not speak English like you or I?" Morgan kept his eyes moving from left to right, checking and re-checking his surroundings. He had to find a way out of the rope as well as food and water.

"No, no. He's not like us at all. I found him here, on this isle. He saved my life and has kept me alive all these years."

"How did you get here, then?" Morgan could feel the uneven surface of the rock behind him. He played his fingers across the hard rock feeling for a jagged edge he could use to cut the ropes. He was only half paying attention to the woman and her incoherent ramblings. She wasn't making sense. If Morgan could get free, he'd use the ropes holding him to tie her up. Then he'd kill the other one. Once they were out of his hair, he could search the cave properly.

"I was born on a ship, lived there with m' father an' mother until he left us on an island somewhere. An occupied island, not like this one. Big. Years passed I got older and one day m' father returned with a ship full of men. The men came into our village, the people I'd grown up with—my friends, and my family. They were pirates, my father and his men. They came, and they killed them all. The pirates had swords. They pretended to be friends with the people of the village, then slaughtered them in the night while they slept. I watch them run from hut to hut, heard the screams in the dark of night. A few of the villagers tried to fight back. They gathered together at the center of the village, m' mother was screaming my name, yelling at me to get back inside until it was over, but I didn't listen to her. I stood at the door to our hut—the hut they left alone —and watched as the villagers charged the pirates. I knew they were m' fathers' men, but I didn't care, I wanted the villagers to kill the pirates. But, of course, they didn't. The pirates were too many. They surrounded the villagers, one of the pirates drew a long sword, pointed the tip of it at one villager then next, he begged them to put down their spears and other weapons. At first the villagers said no, they wouldn't do it. The pirate with the long sword raised it and brought the blade down at an angle. It hit one of the villagers in the neck. The sword almost cut off his head, but not quite. It was my turn to scream into the night as blood spurted up into the air, the villagers around him covered their mouths as the man with the sword in his neck took two steps forward, as if he still wanted to fight."

Morgan stopped feeling around behind him and listened to the woman's story. She wasn't looking at him, just staring down at the ground before her, as if she was telling the story more to herself so she could remember what happened to her than telling it to Morgan. He just happened to be there.

"The pirate reached out and grabbed the impaled man's arm, drew him close," the woman continued. "And then raised his foot, put it on the man's chest and pushed him off the sword. I saw the man crumple to the ground. The pirate laughed as he did this, then he looked at the blade—it was dripping with blood and I could even see pieces of meat falling off it and dropping to the ground—he brought the blade to his mouth and licked it all the way from the hilt to the tip. He looked at the remaining villagers and laughed, they were—like I was—too scared to do anything other than watch. He asked them again to put down their weapons so he didn't have to hurt them. All the villagers dropped their weapons. The pirates looked at each other and laughed, then raised their weapons and killed the rest of the villagers. They drove their swords into their bellies and sliced through arms and legs, they pulled knives and slid them slowly through the villagers' eyes. Even after the villagers were down on the ground, covered in blood and no longer breathing, the pirates continued to hack them up, using anything they could find that was sharp enough to slice off chunks of meat and poke holes into the bodies of the dead. After I'd seen those horrors, m' mother dragged me away from the door and we cowered in the hut, assuming that we would be next."

The woman paused. Morgan didn't know how to respond, so he stayed quiet hoping she would continue. She inhaled long and slow, as if gathering the strength to finish her tale.

"We waited all night in our little hut, m' mother and me. And all night we heard them, laughing and joking around. Then we smelled it. At first, it was just the smoke from the fires, but not long after that, it was the smell of roasting meat. There wasn't much meat in the village or in the surrounding area. We hardly ever ate meat. There was only one place the meat could have come from. My mother peeked out the door a few times, she never told me what she saw, just that I didn't want to know. But I figured it out. The pirates didn't just kill all the villagers, they cooked them and ate them too. They were my friends; they were the adults I looked up to and those men—led by my father—killed them all and then ate them as part of a celebration. When morning came, the fires had stopped, so had the laughing. Everything was silent. My mother stayed awake all night, but I fell asleep. I awoke, my head in my mother's lap and a man standing in the entryway of our hut. At first, I didn't recognize him, but when he said my name, I knew it was my father. I went to him, crying because I was just a kid and didn't know what else to do. He hugged me and beckoned my mother to him. She rose and took his hand then, while I still had my arms wrapped around him in an embrace, he wrapped his hand around her throat and squeezed. She gasped; her eyes wide. She looked—not at my father —but at me. Fear and anger in her face. He squeezed harder, her face turned red then purple as she struggled for air that would not come. I cried and reached for my fathers' arm, but he wouldn't let go of her. Mother's legs kicked out in opposite directions and she collapsed down to the floor. My father dropped to a knee, his hand still squeezing life from her. Her arms and legs twitched and then fell limp on the floor of our hut. He didn't move his hand though, he still held her throat tight in his grip. He was breathing heavy, drool hanging precariously from his bottom lip. I cried. Eventually he pulled away, I thought for sure I was next. He didn't do anything to me though, just left the hut and went back to the ship. I followed him there and cried. He took me on his ship and away from that island. Eventually he brought me here, he told me I could survive on my own here and he would check on me from time to time, but I couldn't stay on his ship any longer. He loved me because I was his daughter, but to a man like that, I guess love meant he simply didn't kill me. That is how I came to be on this isle—and I've been here ever since."

She had reached the conclusion of her story, but Morgan didn't know how to respond and he didn't know what it had to do with having her much larger friend tie him up.

When the silence stretched on, Morgan resumed his search of the wall behind him for any jagged points, but there were none.

"And you've learned to survive here?" Morgan asked.

"He taught me," she said looking, off into the darkness once again. "Saved me, kept me safe, got me food, water, let me live down here with him. I was scared at first, but when he kept me alive it was hard to stay scared. I don't know how long I've been here. Just take it one day at a time. I don't speak in this language anymore. I still think in it, but everything I speak is *his* language."

"He was just here when you arrived?"

"Always been here, as far as I know," she looked away, at the ground, along the wall, anywhere but at Morgan.

"Where is the food and the fresh water?" Morgan said, hoping she'd made some sort of connection with him through the telling of her story.

"The water he gets, some sort of underground spring, I've never seen it. I can't get down there. There's a salt deposit down there too, he says. Never seen that either. The food comes to us." The woman still doesn't look at Morgan even though he makes eye contact throughout the conversation.

"Can he bring me some water? And the food comes to you, do you get a lot of fish off the shore?"

"No. The food is usually up on the beach; we just have to go get it. He gets it usually, but I can get it if we need it."

"I'm not sure why you've tied me up, but I am dying of thirst and could really use some food, too. If you don't want me to see where it is, I understand that. I won't go with you, but please if you could hurry." Morgan knew something was off about her. There was something she wasn't telling him.

"There's a part of the story I guess I forgot to tell you," she said. That smile again grew on one side of her face. She stared into the darkness again, then turned her attention back to Morgan, looking him full in the eyes. He saw happiness there, as if the terrible story she'd just told him had left her mind completely.

9

"I tried fishing off the beach, but there weren't any fish," the woman said. Morgan watched her as she stared into his eyes now. His mouth was dry and his stomach growled, but more than either of those things, he felt weak. He didn't know what dehydration felt like, but he imagined all of his organs drying up at the same time, and he assumed it would feel a lot like the extreme fatigue that had washed over him. He didn't have much time.

"My lover got me water from the spring below, buckets full, but never any food. He let me drink the water, then took my hand and guided me down here. He brought me to the open area where you interrupted us. He left me there and I waited, not knowing what else to do. I stood and waited because I had nowhere else to go and, though I was obviously terrified of him, he seemed like he wanted to help me. So, I waited and he returned not too long after. He had a body with him. A human body. He carried it over his shoulder. I don't know where he got it from or where he stored it, but it was there and though the woman was dead, she appeared to have not been dead very long. He laid her down on the ground, used his long sharp claw and sliced a piece of meat off of her. Then cooked the meat over the fire. Together, we shared her. Since that time, people continue to arrive on our shores, we keep them alive as long as we can, and then, when we need more meat, we kill them and eat them. That is where our food comes from. I've told my story many times, but alas, no one has ever survived to tell it to anyone."

Before Morgan could react to what she was saying, she looked up over him again and the half-smile once again returned to her face, then it grew across her mouth and the leathery yellowed-toothed woman grinned so hard Morgan thought her skin was going to tear from her face. It was only then that he heard the sound of movement to his left.

He turned in time to see the thing with the unpronounceable name. When the woman said the beast was 'not like us,' it was a tremendous understatement. The beast wasn't human and was like nothing Morgan had ever seen. The thing was tall, it stood at least twice as tall as Morgan, but it was crouched and might have been three times as tall as him. The face of the thing was hairless, and pale white, the flat nose and red eyes were the first features Morgan noticed right away. Then the beast opened its mouth, revealing three rows of small but extremely sharp teeth. It growled in Morgan's face, drool dripping out of the tine-filled mouth across Morgan's cheek.

"So-so you're just going to eat me?" Morgan said. For the first time in his life feeling real fear. Even after murdering Jarvis, he didn't feel fear like this. He was expecting what happened on the *Glory*, this was unexpected and inhuman. This was pure fear.

"I'm sorry to say that yes, we will," the woman said, smiling.

The beast picked Morgan up. While its face was pale and hair-less, its body covered in dark matted fur. And the beast smelled horrible, as Morgan was hauled up onto its shoulder, his nose filled with the sickening sweet odor of the beast and it made him gag. Morgan had been aboard a pirate vessel in the middle of summer crossing the Atlantic and the smell wasn't even comparable. This was the worst thing he'd ever smelled—and the woman had called it her lover. The thing's hands were not hands at all, but more like paws with massive claws extending out, they were at least as long as Morgan's forearm.

"But the good news for you is that we already have some freshly cooked meat. So, we will keep you alive a little longer so we can eat you when you're fresh," the woman yelled as the beast carried Morgan away from the fire and into the darkness.

The beast moved fast through the narrowing cave. They turned left and right and took a few more turns inside the dark tunnel before Morgan began to notice the warm light of a small fire once again. There must be ventilation somewhere to keep the fires going and the smoke from building up if they both lived underground, but there wasn't a lot of time for him to dwell on how it all worked. Morgan tried to twist and turn his body to see what was in front of them, but he worried putting up too much of a fight would make the beast angry. After all, the woman said they needed to keep him alive until they ate their last round of meat. It meant more time for Morgan to find a way out of this increasingly difficult situation.

The beast crouched low and rock scraped against Morgan's already cut up back, the beast moved forward and rose back up to almost it's full height. The ground was a long way down and the beast had stopped moving forward, it just held Morgan high above the hard stone floor.

"Just put me down," Morgan said, unable to remember if the woman said her lover could understand him or not. "Easy, easy."

The rock surrounding him swung fast. Morgan realized he was being whipped down toward the ground. He braced himself for the impact of unforgiving stone against his back and skull. He was surprised when instead of the hard landing he was expecting, the landing was soft and there was hardly any impact at all. Morgan scrambled around and managed to get up on all fours. The beast looked down at him; the pale skin and reddish-pink eyes of the thing glared down at him—not in anger though, instead it was a look of uncaring, almost as if Morgan wasn't worth the monster's time. Morgan worked himself to his feet and gave a quick look around. He was in a small room somewhere inside the cave. There was only one way out, and it was blocked by the beast. Morgan thought about his next move but only for a moment, he decided if he was going to get out of there, he was going to have to go through the beast, so he sprinted toward it, but before he could get close enough to the small entrance to the room he was in, a massive boulder slid into place, blocking the only way out. There was a small crack at the top of the opening just wide enough for Morgan to push his hand through, but that was it.

"No!" Morgan shouted into the vast cave, but it was too late. The beast had already left. Precious little light leaked into the room from the small space at the top of the opening. The fire Morgan had seen must have been just outside the room.

He leaned against the rock and tried to push it, but it wouldn't move. He was weak from lack of food and water, but certain, even if he was at full strength, he would not have been able to move the huge boulder. He'd traded a cell on the *Glory* for a cell in a cave. He preferred the cell on the ship, all things being equal.

For a while there were no sounds other than the occasional crackle from the fire on the other side of the boulder. Then the tapping and scraping sound of claws against stone echoed around him. He hadn't been inside the chamber for very long, maybe the beast was just walking past. But Morgan heard a second sound—a quiet, low shuffling sound had joined the tapping against the rock.

Both noises got louder, closer, then stopped.

"We got ya some water," the woman's voice called from the other side of the boulder.

Tremors shook his hands at the thought of water. He didn't realize how much he needed the water until then.

"Alright, thank you," even his voice quivered as he spoke.

"Get your face as close as you can to that opening, he's going to pour it in slowly, not sure how much you'll get, but it's the only way to get you any water and keep you feeling good. Just open up and he'll start pouring. There's a whole bucket here for you, just tell me if you need a break and I'll have him stop."

Morgan stood up and was just tall enough to get his mouth right at the small opening at the top of the boulder, he opened his mouth, feeling like a baby bird waiting for a meal, but he didn't care. He needed the water badly; it was all he could think about.

"I'm ready," Morgan said. The woman said something to the beast that sounded like she was clearing her throat and spitting on the floor of the cave. A moment of silence and more movement and shuffling echoed from the opposite side of the boulder, then water came. It came slowly, like she'd promised, but it was still too much for Morgan to handle all at once. It poured in the room along the top of the boulder, Morgan moved his mouth to catch the falling water and got a mouthful, which he gulped down. The beast kept pouring and Morgan grabbed a second mouthful, swallowing that as well. Cold, fresh water slipped into his throat, down his gullet, and sloshed around inside his stomach. He realized he was getting over-full. If he kept gulping, he would vomit it all up. He'd gone too long putting nothing inside his stomach and needed to drink and eat slowly.

"That's enough," Morgan gasped, even as his mouth searched for more. He could have had another three or four mouthfuls, but he knew his stomach couldn't handle it. It took all of his willpower not to ask for more.

"We can get ya some food too, just wait there," the woman shouted to him.

"Alright." Morgan wiped water and drool from his chin. He laid down and caught his breath, propping his head up with a hand against his forehead.

Once he caught his breath, he turned and slid himself over to the boulder preventing his exit from the cave. He found the cool wet spot on the stone floor and rested his face in a puddle of water.

10

"Hello," the woman's voice woke him through the darkness. It reached into his slumber and pulled him from it. At first, Morgan wasn't quite sure where he was. "Hello, you in there. You told me your name but I don't remember it, you awake?"

Morgan sat up, his cheek still wet from the puddle he'd slept in.

"Yes, yes I'm awake. I'm Edward. Edward Morgan."

"Right, right. Edward, you told me that before didn't ya? I threw some food in there for ya. Gotta fatten you up."

Morgan looked around and found a few scraps of dried meat. He knew it was human meat and so didn't pick it up right away, even as his stomach rolled and felt like it was beginning to digest itself.

"Yes, thank you." Morgan sat up and leaned with his back against the rock. "Listen, I think you might be making a mistake fattening me up or killing me for food."

"Oh ya? Why d'ya say that? Almost everyone begs us not to eat them at some point or another. I always like ta find out exactly what the reason is. If there's a good reason, well then maybe we won't eat you right away, but I've never heard a good reason yet."

"Well, not everyone is me. Trust me, you're going to let me out of here when you hear what I have to say."

"Well, come on and let me hear what it is then."

"Alright. I was on a ship, the *Glory*, you remember me telling you that? I told you they just left me here to die." Morgan said, hoping the promise of more food would be enough for her. "Well, that's not completely true. They ship didn't sink. The Captain of the *Glory*— he told me he'd be back, because he thought I have the ability to survive here. I don't know if he knew about the two of you—I don't think he did—but anyway. He said he'd come back, pick me up if I was still alive in twenty days. I don't know how many days I've been down here in this cave, maybe two or three? But I spent one day exploring the isle. So, it's been seventeen days now at most. When they come, if they see me, they'll get close enough to pick me up. When they do, you and your—your friend—can take the ship, I'll help you, then you'll have lots of men, lots of meat. There are over fifty men on that ship. And you can eat them all. Plus, the ship has rations, you could eat the dried fruit and anything else on the ship."

There was a long silence, it stretched on, Morgan thought maybe the woman left before she even heard the story, but then she responded, "That's the best story I heard yet. All of that true?"

"Completely true."

"Well, then, let me talk to him. You eat up though, either way you're going to need some food."

The woman shuffled away and Morgan stared at the dried human meat on the floor. He didn't want to eat it. He wasn't sure—even if he got it in his mouth—he would be able to chew it and swallow it down. Putting the remains of a human in your mouth was one thing, actually swallowing a person's remains was another thing entirely.

At the protests of his stomach, which had tied itself into a tight knot, he eventually picked up the meat and held it in his hand. The idea of eating the jerky made him gag, but his stomach didn't care, it had been three days without food, possibly more, his stomach was looking for anything it could digest, it didn't care if it was the arse or arm of another person.

Morgan sat and turned the meat over in his hand, wondering

exactly where on the person it had come from. Eating dried beef, he never questioned where the meat had come from. Meat was meat. Unless it was human meat.

Luckily, the familiar shuffling and scratching sound grew before Morgan's stomach won the battle and he ate his meal. Instead, he dropped it on the ground and stood up.

"You ate up like I told ya?" The woman sounds louder, happier. Maybe it was a good sign.

"Ah, yes, I did."

"I can tell that means you didn't. You better eat up though. If we were just gonna eat you, I might let you go without eatin'. Eventually you'd get hungry enough in there that you'd take a bite of that meat, or you'd die. But since we're keeping you alive to get the rest of your friends here, you're going to have to eat and be strong enough to help us. If you don't eat, we'll force you to eat. Or he can just crush your skull. I'd rather have fresh meat, but if we have to dry you all up, we'll still survive."

"So, you're going to let me live?" Morgan had another reprieve. He didn't know how long it would last, all he had to do was stay alive long enough to figure out his next step.

"For now. We like the idea of a ship full of people, instead of just picking up one person here and there. We have had some lean times over the years when there was not much to eat. This would help get us through the lean times."

Morgan smiled to himself. He'd get the ship here, let that monster take as many of the people on the ship as it could, and then Morgan could take the *Glory* for himself when no one was looking. He just had to figure out how he was going to pull it off. As long as he got the woman and her monster to trust him, he was going to succeed. He knew it.

"You should let me out of here then, so we can plan. If they get suspicious, they will just leave. Whatever we do, it has to look like I survived here on my own this whole time. If not, they won't get close enough to the isle. Can your friend swim?" Morgan's mind was already churning. He didn't have a plan yet, but one was beginning to form.

"We're going to let you out. You seem like someone we can trust, but you gotta listen to us. You gotta listen to me, or you're going back in. We have a deal?"

"I am honest. I will work with you and we all get what we all want. You have a deal."

After a few minutes, the beast moved the boulder out of the way and Morgan and the woman were facing each other once again. The pieces of dried meat lay on the floor of the room.

"One last thing, I need you ta eat that. Not just to keep you alive. So, we know you're really with us, too. We've never brought someone else in with us like this. We want to make sure you're just like us. Eating that human meat, it changes a person. That night when I smelled the meat cooking from the villagers, I didn't realize it then, but something changed in me. I didn't even eat it that night, but I knew I could if I had to. And I did, to survive here. I keep surviving here because of how that day changed me. So, eat, feel the change, then we can move on."

She stood just inside the opening, the dim light barely reached in because behind her, the massive beast blocked the rest of the opening. The boulder was out of the way, but it was clear Morgan wasn't free until he ate.

It would be okay. It wasn't going to change him; he didn't believe the words she'd said. She was a crazy woman who lived alone on an island with a huge monster. She might be a cannibal, but she didn't know what she was talking about. He'd eat it because they forced him to, because he needed to eat it to stay alive, not because he was an actual cannibal.

Morgan held the meat, turned it again a few times in his hands.

"Go on now, it's not gonna kill ya, I promise. Just change ya."

Morgan sucked in a long slow breath and held it. He closed his eyes and imagined this was all over. He was aboard the *Glory* in his mind. He stood at the helm with a handful of crew with him. The rest of them were on the isle with the woman and her monster.

They were the food, they were the ones sentenced to death. And Morgan was free. All he had to do to get out of the cave was eat the food.

With his eyes still closed, he raised the human meat to his mouth and pushed it in. He gagged only once, just as he started chewing.

"There you are," the woman said.

Morgan finished chewing, it was not salty, but the flavor was very near to that of beef. He swallowed.

It was done. He didn't realize it then, but the woman was right, it changed him.

11

"I think I should learn your name if we're going to be working together," Morgan said after he'd left the small room with the woman and the beast. The beast walked in front, the narrow hallways of the cave made it impossible for them to walk shoulder to shoulder, so the monstrous thing led the way, followed by the woman and then Morgan. The halls of the cave were not just narrow, they were dark too, so Morgan stayed very close to the woman, not wanting to get lost in the dark labyrinth below Dead Mans Isle.

The woman laughed, but it sounded more like a short, loud cough. "I haven't had a name since my father left me here that day I told you about. You wanna use the name that they used to call me, that's fine. He just uses his word for female, you can call me that, or Annie, if ya want."

"Annie, then. I'll call you Annie. Did your mother name you?" Morgan asked, he was genuinely curious and wanted to know more. Plus, he was developing a soft spot for her. She hadn't done anything other than try to survive here. Maybe he could get her to leave with him.

Annie gave him the same laugh-cough then turned to look back at him.

"You got about as much back story as you're gonna get. You were a few weeks away from being my dinner, so I'm not gonna turn around and be your friend now. We're just working together to get what we need. Then we're done."

"Have it your way," Morgan said. He wasn't going to push the issue now, but he'd always had a way with women and was determined to get her guard down. He still had time.

They reached the open area where Morgan first encountered Annie and the beast after traversing the cave from the surface. Annie invited him to sit by the fire, which he did, and the beast sat as well. The fire was burning hot but there was not much flame, so the light was low.

As they sat, Morgan felt the beast's eyes on him. He refused to return the creature's glare though. He feared the monster, but didn't want to give it the satisfaction of seeing his fear, so Morgan was determined to sit as if he didn't care one way or the other what the beast was doing. Showing confidence—even if it was faux-confidence—could only help him in the long run.

"What time is it?" Morgan asked, exhaustion finally hitting him. Now that he had water and food in his stomach, the stress of what he'd been through since arriving on the island was starting to wear on him.

"Doesn't matter that much," Annie replied. "We don't go to the surface. So, it's always dark. We eat when we're hungry, sleep when we're tired, and we keep ourselves busy the rest of the time." She looked at the beast, the half-smile stretched across her mouth.

Morgan pushed the image of the two of them fecking out of his mind. He didn't even know how it would be physically possible. The size of the beast and her small, frail frame, he couldn't—and didn't want to—picture it.

"I understand," Morgan said. "But we must keep track of time to be ready for when the ship arrives. I need to be ready for them, and so do the two of you. I know you came up and saw me sleeping. So, you do come up from time to time. If I'm up there, I'll be able to keep track of the days. I'll know approximately when the *Glory* will be back. If we know when they are coming it will be an advantage for us. Also, if they come back early and I'm not up there, well, then we lose our chance."

"And you go back to being our dinner, don't you Edward." Annie unleashed her hacking laugh.

"Right," Morgan forced out a smile, wondering if he should help her or if she'd be better off staying on the isle with the beast. He looked to the beast, wondering if the thing could understand what they were saying, but it just sat there, its legs curled up underneath it more like a cat or dog than a human "But none of us want that, which is why I think it would be best to let me stay up there during the day, and then come down to sleep and eat with you two at night. What do you think?"

Annie looked at her massive lover and then began making noises from the back of her throat. The beast tilted its head and made a deep, guttural noise back at her. The sound of its voice rumbled the stone around them. Annie spoke back to him and they continued on in conversation a few more minutes. Morgan did his best to read Annie's face as they talked, trying to determine exactly what they were talking about and what the decision would be. They were supposed to be working together, but it was clear the beast—and by proxy, Annie—was still in charge of the situation.

The beast turned its pale head, the sharp pink eyes stared at Morgan and the thing let out a low growl and bared its teeth at him. An overwhelming desire to run overtook Morgan and he almost fled the cave. He could see the path leading up out of the rock and onto the isle above, it wouldn't take much for him to get there. But the beast was too fast. Morgan remained still, avoiding eye-contact with the beast until the growling stopped. The beast closed its mouth and put its head back down, resting it on heavy, clawed paws. Then the beast looked at Annie and snorted, Annie burst out with another laugh, this time the coughing aspect of it was absent. As if those other laughs had been fake and this one more genuine.

"He's teasing you," she smiled a full smile at Morgan, then glanced side-eyed at the beast. "We think it's alright if you spend most of your time up there. Not like you can go anywhere. One of us will come up and check on you and bring you food and water every day. If you want to sleep down here with us, you can, just know that many nights we do more than just sleep. Either way you'll get food and water every day. And we will be ready when your friends get here."

"Alright," Morgan said. He stood up, he wanted to see if it was day or night, he wanted to breathe in the fresh air because the stench in the cave—while he was getting used to it—was still close to unbearable.

"You're one of us now," Annie muttered as he stood.

"What do you mean?"

The beast growled again; this growl was different. Morgan sensed real anger this time.

"That meat you ate earlier, it was from the thigh of an overweight man. He was older than you and smelled like rotting fish when he was alive. He was much larger than you and so we got a lot more meat from him. Just think, if he was skinnier we'd be hungry and you wouldn't be standing there right now."

"I—" Morgan started, but Annie wasn't done.

"Only reason we're willing to try this out is because we've got enough meat for the three of us until your friends come back. *If* they come back. My point was, you are one of us now. A cannibal. That man's thigh is rolling around inside your belly right now and makin' you stronger. You got a taste of human meat and you'll never be the same."

Morgan's stomach clenched, he felt the bile begin to rise up and burn the back of his throat, but he choked it back down.

"I'll be up there, on the beach I was on the other night when you need to check on me."

With that, Morgan spun on his heel and found the tunnel to the surface.

There was waning daylight when Morgan stepped out of the

hole in the middle of the isle. He scanned the area around him and it was just as he'd left it a day or two earlier. He looked up at the two trees flanking the opening, got his bearings and began the short walk back to the beach. He'd sleep well knowing the only two living things on the isle were actually under the isle. And though they were a hideous man-eating monster and his cannibal female lover, they were on his side for the time being and so he felt cautiously safe.

There was something different about him though, maybe Annie had been right. When he stepped down into the hole in the ground, he'd never tasted human flesh—never wanted to—that was no longer the case. Stepping in the hole had saved his life, but at what cost? His stomach was full and it was enough to make him drowsy, so he couldn't put much thought into the fact that he'd become a cannibal down there. Once he was off the isle, hopefully with Annie, and leaving the beast and most of the crew of the *Glory* dead in his wake, he could figure out how to deal with the changes that had occurred in him here.

Morgan found the spot on the beach where he'd slept and lay down, his body relaxed as soon as his head hit the sand. He was asleep within minutes.

12

Bright sun in his face and the gentle splash of waves against sand woke him. Morgan rolled onto his side and clutched his seizing stomach. He gagged, felt the vomit building in his gut, but nothing came out. He gagged a second time, this time rising himself up on his knees fully expecting a greenish yellow jet of bile to spurt out and splash against the sand. Still, there was nothing. It was his body reacting to the meat. He knew it, but worse, he knew Annie—or the beast—would be up today with more meat for him. His stomach would not get a reprieve.

However, knowing a steady source of food and water was coming, shifted his priorities. Before it had been about food and water, now it was about finding a way to kill the beast and convince Annie to go with him. He had to get her to realize that the isle was not the best place for her. He knew it made him look weak, but he'd developed a soft spot for her. She reminded him too much of his mother. If he could kill the beast, she would either go with him willingly, or try to kill him. There was no in between. But killing the beast wouldn't be easy, if it was even possible at all. He had food in his stomach and had drunk enough that he felt full. He was going to get more water today and more food, most likely.

Morgan decided to save half the meat he was given each day, to build up a supply so he wouldn't have to rely on Annie and the beast to provide him with those things.

He also wanted to save the water, if possible, but it seemed a little harder than just stashing a piece of dried meat away for a few days. And he was going to find something sharp he could use as a weapon.

Morgan stood up, the sand had been soft when he first lay down, but now, after a night of sleeping, it was hard and unforgiving. He brushed off his clothes and then gazed at the blue water stretched out before him. The cuts along his back still ached at times, but mostly, he barely noticed them. The salt water had helped with the healing. Morgan stripped off his clothes, leaving them in a pile on top of a small rock and stepped into the water. It felt cool on his skin as he washed away the sweat and grime of the cave. He dunked himself underwater and then rose up, letting the sun dry him as he walked back up to the beach. He searched around the beach for a sharp rock as he strolled.

"You're a healthy-looking man, if I do say," Annie's voice cut the silence. Morgan jumped, he hadn't seen her approach. If he'd found a weapon, he might have used it out of reflex. Good thing for her, he hadn't.

Morgan made no move to cover himself, he smiled at her and then laughed.

"Been awhile since you've been with an actual man, has it Annie?" He still wanted to get her on his side.

"Never," Annie said, her gaze shifting from Morgan's body to the ocean beyond.

"He's all I've ever known. Never been with a man, only with him."

"Do you wish things could be different?" Morgan grabbed at his clothes and pulled them on.

"No," Annie smiled and stared out at the ocean once again. "Maybe one time, long ago, I wished for a different life. But I've gotten used to this. This is my life now."

"Sounds like you don't want it to be this way though. Annie, it's not too late to change your life." Morgan knew he was taking a chance, but he had a feeling he was reading this woman correctly. She only lived like this because there was no alternative. She'd jump at the chance to get off the isle, Morgan trusted himself. You couldn't get anything in life without taking a chance. "Annie, leave with me. When the ship comes, we can leave. We can leave the entire crew here for—your friend—we will take care of him. Then you can come on the ship with me. We can leave this place behind. Find you a *new* life. You don't have to be defined by your past and by what you saw when you were a girl. You can be different. No one but me will ever know."

Annie was silent. He watched her. Her face softened and she looked out at the open ocean. A smile crossed her lips. There was something in her eye. A glint, a hope, a dream of something different. She was buying it.

Then just as quickly, her face hardened once again. Her mouth became a tight line. Her eyes went from light blue and alive to grey and cold.

"No. I can't. That life is over. If you ever bring that up again, our deal is off and I'll be chewing on that nice body of yours for dinner. Maybe I'll even cut the pieces off of you while you're still alive, make you watch me eat you. Maybe I'll even let you eat some of yourself before you die. Don't talk about that anymore with me. I could never leave him. *Never!*"

"I understand, I don't want any of that to happen. I wasn't trying to push. I just was thinking, maybe in all these years you haven't had the opportunity to get off the isle. But now you might. I won't talk about this anymore with you." Morgan didn't need to say anything else. He'd seen her face; he'd seen the doubt and the wondering there. He would have to pull back for the time being. As the day approached, he'd give it another shot.

"I brought you some food and some water," Annie nodded toward the bucket and stack of three pieces of dried meat sitting next to it on the sand. "We have three buckets, we'll bring one up and take the empty one back down every day and we'll still have one for us."

Morgan nodded. Annie turned and left without another word. He watched her until she got to the center of the isle and disappeared into the cave.

Once she was gone, Morgan finished dressing and sat on the ground next to his food and water. The bucket was about half full, he touched the damp wood to his lips, wondering how Annie was able to fashion it without any type of axe or sharp edge. Then he thought of the beast's sharp claws. He shivered. With two hands gripping the bucket tightly, he tipped it back and let the cool water run into his mouth and down his throat. He could have drunk it all at once, but he held back, took a breath, filled his mouth once more and put the bucket down. The bucket was still more than a quarter full. If he didn't find something to hold the fresh water in, he would drink the rest later on.

Feeling more energized from the water, Morgan stood up. He looked down at the three pieces of dried human meat sitting next to the bucket. His stomach rumbled at the thought of food, but he wasn't sure he could force down another bite of the stuff. Instead of eating, Morgan turned and scoured the beach for anything that might work to hold the water for him. There were no large indentations on the rocks that would work, and the leaves of the small bushes were too small to be of any use. His only chance would be to get Annie and the beast's bucket, but if that happened, they'd stop bringing him water. Things were going to have to stay as they were until they were closer to the return of the *Glory*.

Morgan returned to the food and water empty handed. He looked down again at the human meat and his stomach once again let him know it was time to eat. Morgan exhaled, closed his eyes, and picked up the top piece of meat. It was the largest of the three, and Morgan tried not to visualize what portion of the man he was about to ingest. He opened his mouth, placed the meat on his tongue, and began chewing, tasting the meat. He gagged, but it was not as bad as it had been the first time. Morgan swallowed and, before he knew it, the entire piece of dried meat was gone.

The other two pieces of meat still sat on the ground next to him. Morgan picked them up and brought them to a small bush just at the edge of the beach. With his hands, he dug a hole in the sand at its base and buried the meat there. Just in case Annie and the beast stopped feeding him.

He did not see Annie or the beast for the rest of the day.

13

The process repeated itself every day for the next five days. Morgan woke and searched a different part of the isle for something sharp he could use as a weapon against the beast—and just in case—Annie. Usually, by the time he returned—empty handed—from his search, Annie was there with a bucket and a few pieces of meat for him. Morgan had yet to find a place to store the fresh water, so she took the empty bucket and left a new, full bucket for him.

The two of them hardly spoke. Either Annie was still mad at him for talking to her about leaving this place, or she was secretly contemplating taking him up on the offer. He doubted though, that she'd told her beast-lover about his proposition yet.

Morgan was content to let her return to the cave without a word.

On the sixth morning, everything changed.

Morgan realized he'd been living off of one piece of meat for the last six days. Even though he felt the hunger running through him, he wasn't weak and knew he could continue to live off one piece a day until the *Glory* returned. Doing some quick math, he recognized he'd saved up enough food to survive on one piece a day until the ship returned. He still didn't have fresh water, but he didn't need to rely on the beast or Annie for food. It was a start. If he could get two full buckets of water, he could probably make it last. He still didn't know what to do about Annie. He'd make one more plea to her. He didn't want to hurt her if he didn't have to. She was still a threat to him, maybe he could tie her up, but he still had to get rid of the beast.

Taking out the beast wouldn't be easy, but Morgan would have the element of surprise on his side and might be able to pull it off.

When Annie brought his food and water, Morgan thanked her, as he had done every day. When she turned back to the cave, Morgan stopped her.

"Do you think I could come down there for a while, just to get out of the sun for an hour or two?"

At first, Annie didn't turn around. She stood with her back to him motionless. Then, without turning around, gave her answer.

"No one's making ya stay up here. You can come down if ya want. Stay up here if ya want. I'm going back now," her piece said, she headed back toward the cave. Morgan eyed a large rock off to his right. He'd tested its weight before and knew he could hold it in one hand. It would have been easy to grab the rock, run up behind Annie and collapse her skull in. He didn't want to do it. The end was so close, though. Was killing Annie worth it? He didn't know what to do. He needed that second bucket of water first.

"Alright. I will eat and drink and be down."

Annie said nothing else and returned to the cave. Once she had dropped below ground and out of his sight, Morgan picked up the fist-sized rock and made his way there himself. His heart was pounding. He'd been doing nothing but sitting around looking for weapons, drinking and eating human meat for almost a week. It was time to jump into action.

When Morgan got to the entrance of the cave, he was ready. He'd played out the scene a million times in his head over the last few days, he needed to get the bucket of water first. Killing the beast wouldn't be easy, but Morgan had confidence in his abilities. Maybe too much confidence. He exhaled, shook his head, then stepped off the sandy soil and down onto the rock floor of the cave.

Morgan took his time traversing the tunnel down into the earth for the second time. His first time going down he was curious about what lay ahead, on his way out he was more worried about getting the hell out of the cave. This time, he was more calculated. He knew what lay ahead, and he could take his time and look for weapons along the way. A few steps down, he stopped and gently placed the rock against the wall of the cave. He wanted to have it close by just in case. Then he kept moving forward, darkness slowly overtaking him. He kept his eyes down as he walked, but there were no weapons or stray rocks littering the path. It was clear. As far as he could remember, it was the same as it had been his first time down.

Dim light appeared out of the darkness ahead, Morgan knew he was getting close to the opening and the wide-open chamber where he'd first encountered his isle mates.

The first time he'd heard Annie speaking in that strange, beast-voice. This time, he heard something different entirely.

He wasn't sure what he was listening to. It was Annie, but she was not making the same sounds he'd heard before. Morgan took another few steps, Annie's breath was rapid, almost as if she was in pain. He thought he knew what he heard, then, when Annie gasped and let out a loud, high-pitched moan, Morgan knew exactly what he was happening. He couldn't help but smile. He moved closer wanting to see exactly how she managed quiffing with the giant beast.

He assumed seeing them go at it, would be amusing. Morgan had snuck around as a kid watching the men get in bed with the prosti-tutes that lived in the house down the street when he was growing up. When he was older, kids had poked their heads in to see him doing the same thing, it had all been in good fun. Everyone felt good so what was the harm, right? It wasn't like the woman was some-one's mother; just a prostitute. So, when Morgan heard Annie getting a rogering from the beast, he was transported back to his youth. He thought there would be nothing wrong. That it would all be in good fun. But he was wrong. What he saw made him re-think everything.

He moved closer, keeping to the shadows as much as possible. Their backs were mostly to him, either of them would have had to crane their neck back at an awkward position to see him. Though Morgan was certain Annie would not be moving her head.

She was naked and folded in half across a rock jutting up from the cave floor. It wasn't a flat rock though, so while her feet were touching the ground on one side, her hands were holding herself up on the other with the point of the rock pressing into her abdomen. The gigantic beast was on top of her, pressing Annie down into the point of the rock.

Morgan shuffled closer, moving slowly, so he didn't make any noise, not that either of them would have heard him over Annie's constant moaning. He crouched behind another nearby rock and watched, horrified by what he was seeing, but unable to turn away.

The beast was behind Annie, but crouched down because she was obviously much too short for him to stand behind her. His body was pressed against her, his plugtail—no doubt huge as well— buried somewhere deep inside her. The beast's giant forepaws were against her back and on the back of her head, claws pressed hard against her skin. The beast looked forward, snarling and drooling down on Annie's back as he pushed himself into her over and over.

Her body rocked back and forth and slammed against the hard stone with each of the beast's brutal thrusts. The beast increased his speed and the sound of their bodies slapping together echoed throughout the cave. He growled down at her, her legs quivering and shaking, barely able to hold up to the constant pounding. She turned her head and the light from the fire hit it just right, Morgan could see her face for only a moment. It was a mixture of sadness and pain. There was no pleasure in her face at all. This was different from any time Morgan had laid with a woman or any of the shite he saw through the windows of the house down the street as a kid. Annie said the beast was her lover, but this was not loving—even to

Morgan who was not a gentle lover—this was violence. And it only got worse.

The beast dug its claws into Annie's back, penetrating her body in more than one place. Blood pooled around the places where the claws dug in, then it dripped down her body. A combination of saliva and blood trickled down her back, along her ribs and then dripped onto the dark stone floor of the cave. He dragged the sharp points down, opening up long but not very deep cuts from the bottom of her neck to her lower back. Morgan winced, thinking of his own—now mostly healed—cuts. He wondered how often the beast cut her like that.

The beast growled, its massive body towering over Annie's small, delicate frame. The thrusting grew harder and faster, and Annie's moans of pleasure had long since become screams of pain. The beast howled when Annie began to squirm underneath. She turned her head again, her eyes shut tight, tears streaming down her cheeks. She wasn't a lover, she was a prisoner, just like Morgan. He felt a change in him, he'd get her out of this, situation one way or another.

The beast's climax was coming, fur covered muscle slammed into delicate flesh again and again. The beast howled—even louder than before. Morgan crouched down and covered his ears with his hands, wondering how Annie was able to bear it. More blood dripped from her, the beast howled and raised its massive head up into the air, almost scraping it against the ceiling of the open chamber. The movement stopped. The beast held Annie still under his weight, then withdrew himself from her, his plug-tail hung limp and massive. Blood and fluid from the beast dripped out of Annie. Morgan wondered how she was still breathing. The howling ceased. Only Annie's soft panting could be heard. The beast lowered himself. Once its paws were off Annie and its claws no longer digging into her skin, the beast bent his head and began to lap at her back, licking up the blood as it seeped out of the cuts he'd placed there.

Morgan ducked back behind the rock so he was completely out

of sight. He wished he'd just stayed on the beach. He didn't need to see any of this. If he'd stayed on the beach, he'd still look at Annie as the enemy. Now it was hard to think of her that way. She'd been brainwashed by the beast all these years. Brainwashed and ravaged. The beast had needs, and there was nothing else around for it to feck, so when Annie showed up, the beast took a liking to her. She needed to get off the isle as much as Morgan did. But getting her to turn her back on the beast was going to be hard and going to make Morgan's own escape much harder. One way or another, he was going to save her from this. Morgan might have been an arsehole with a bad attitude, but he also loved his mother and remembered what his father did to her. He knew abuse when he saw it.

14

The beast disappeared into the darkness, as he had the first time Morgan walked in on them. The first time the pair had just been talking, this time it was something more brutal.

He waited in the darkness. He'd told Annie he was eating and then coming down here. Did she know he was watching? Did she care? Did she have any say at all in when or where the beast had her? Morgan didn't think so.

Annie lay unmoving. Morgan didn't move either. He waited and watched. She had been through this before and probably needed to recover after what had just happened to her. It was a long time, if the cave hadn't been so silent, Morgan would have snuck back to the surface and stayed there, never bothering to return. But if he moved, or even breathed too loudly, Annie would hear him for certain.

A long time passed; Morgan worried the beast would return. If he did and saw Annie still folded across the rock like that, would he give her another go? It was a possibility; Morgan did not want to witness the act a second time. He resolved to count to one hundred and if Annie didn't move, he would take his chances, back up slowly, and leave the cave.

He only got to twenty-seven when Annie groaned, pushed herself up and then off the rock. She collapsed down on the hard stone cave floor, her face flat against the stone, her arms curled up underneath her. Her naked body lay prone, almost like a child, the gashes on her back still dripping and oozing.

She didn't stay there long, she sat up and pushed her hair out of her face.

"Enjoy the show, did ya?" She spoke in the darkness.

"Annie, I'm sorry, I-I didn't know," Morgan whispered. He stood up and began to walk toward her, then wondered if he should and stopped.

"I knew you were coming, I thought you might want to see what our relationship is really like. It's love." Annie rose to her feet, blood dripped from her back and from in-between her legs.

"Why let him do that to you? It's clear it's painful."

"Looks worse than it is," Annie made no attempt to cover herself. If he hadn't just witnessed the brutal act, Morgan might have found himself aroused by her.

"It didn't look like love. It looked terrible. Annie, let me get you away from here. Come with me," Morgan spoke as quietly as he could. Annie said the beast couldn't understand English, but Morgan had seen evidence that proved he knew at least some of the language, he didn't want to take any chances.

"I told ya I wasn't going and that's what I'm doing. Don't ask again," she said.

Morgan exhaled, if she was going to come with him, he'd have to take her against her will. He couldn't leave her in this situation.

"I won't ask again. It is possible for me to get another bucket of water, Annie. I spilled most of the one you just brought. Since I'm here and there is plenty of water. I will bring both buckets back when they are empty so you don't have to make a second trip."

Annie sighed and hobbled over to the barely lit fire. On the other side of the protruding rocks was a bucket. She hefted it up and brought it to him.

"Might as well. He went to get more water and food for us. The spring is far down there. I've never been that far in, he can see just as well in daylight as he can in the dark, so it's easy for him to travel down there and get a bucketful. The food is down there too because the smell is pretty bad when the meat starts to rot. He doesn't mind it, but I can't be in here if it's too close, so it stays far enough away that the smell doesn't reach me."

Annie placed the bucket at Morgan's feet. She stood and looked at him, the blood pooling under her.

"Thank you," was all Morgan said. He watched the blood collect at her feet.

"It's what we do. It doesn't hurt bad and it's been going on a long time. Thank ya for your concern, but I'm fine," she said finally. Then quickly, as if embarrassed, "now no more talk of it. It's done."

Morgan nodded, turned his back on the naked, bloody woman and left the cave.

There was no time to dwell on what he'd seen. If Annie wanted to let the beast feck her and tear her apart, he would allow it. But he'd still try to figure out a way to save her from that beast. His own survival was still his top priority and he'd managed to come away from the cave with a second bucket of water. He had enough food and water now to last him until the *Glory* returned.

He wanted to help Annie, but also didn't need her to survive any longer. If she got in his way, he'd have a hard choice to make.

Morgan returned to the beach and hid both buckets of water. He'd make one final appeal to Annie in the morning.

15

Morgan didn't put his head down to sleep that night. He rested his eyes and sat up against the rock face like he had the first night he'd been on Dead Man's Isle after Annie—or maybe it was the beast— woke him up. He needed to be awake and ready for Annie well before she arrived from the cave with his daily ration of food and water. If he wasn't ready and she didn't see two empty buckets of water, she might suspect something, return to the cave and alert the beast. He needed to surprise the beast if he had any chance against it.

He was up and ready before the sun the next morning. He had the fist-sized rock in his hand. Annie usually took the same path from the cave to his beach, so he'd hide out of sight as best he could and come up behind her. He wanted to be between her and the cave when he broached the subject of leaving with him one last time. He couldn't have her running back to the beast to alert him. If she still wasn't open to going with him, he would have to knock her out and tie her up.

There was a thick bush with a lot of leaves about halfway between the cave and the beach. Morgan hid himself behind the bush so he'd be out of Annie's line of sight, but he'd still be able to watch her through the leaves. When she passed by the bush, he'd come up behind her.

He waited a long time.

Eventually, the sun rose up in yet another cloudless day. The same weather as every other day since he'd arrived. It was going to be hot, and it was going to be dry. Morgan continued to flex one leg, then the other to keep the circulation in his legs. He needed to be ready to move at a moment's notice.

Then he saw her. His eyes had been glued to the area between the two trees for so long, he almost didn't realize it was Annie when she came up out of the cave. But she was there, the same as always: bucket of water in one hand, dried human meat in the other.

Morgan grabbed his rock and gripped it tightly in his right hand as he crouched down further behind the bush. There was no way she could see him from that distance, but he needed to remain still as she made her approach. She got closer to the bush, and then finally moved past it. As she did, Morgan circled around the bush, keeping its thick leaves between Annie and himself. When she was at least twenty or thirty paces beyond the bush, he came out from his hiding spot. He followed her, keeping each step as noiseless as possible. When Annie got to the edge of the beach, she looked to her left and then to her right, at the small cliff. She didn't turn back. Morgan wasn't sure if she knew he was there or not.

"Where are you?" Annie shouted to the empty beach. She put the bucket of water down in the sand and Morgan jumped at the chance. He sprinted up behind her, closing the five steps between them with only two quick strides. Morgan wrapped his arm around her throat and pulled her back against him. He held the rock above her head and leaned in close to her ear.

"Last chance, Annie. I don't think it's safe for you to be here. I'm getting off this isle and I'm going to kill that beast before I do it. I don't want to hurt you, but I can't have you letting him know I'm coming either."

Annie laughed, it was the hacking, cough-like laugh Morgan had heard from her before.

"I knew you were up to something yesterday when you wanted more water. I didn't think you'd come after us this fast. You're a crazy one that's for sure. I told you I'm not changing my mind." Annie didn't fight him off and didn't make any attempt to yell for help. Morgan thought he had the upper hand, but he was confused. "We kept an eye on you, just in case. He's been up here with you all night and been watching you all day, too. Should only be a matter of seconds now before he crushes your skull. Looks like I'll be eating you after all."

Morgan panicked and pushed Annie away. He looked around, expecting the giant beast to jump at him and attack him. He'd only released Annie for a second before she sprinted past him, back toward the cave, her cackle like a lightning bolt through the otherwise stagnant air.

The beast wasn't there, she'd tricked him. And he'd fallen for it. He had to stop her, even if it meant hurting her. He didn't want to, but she'd left him no choice.

She was fast and had a head start on him. Morgan sprinted after her, he pumped his arms and held the stone tight in his right hand. He was gaining on her, but the two trees were getting close, he wasn't sure he was going to catch her in time.

Annie started yelling before she reached the opening to the cave. She was yelling the beast's name and some other words Morgan didn't recognize, but he didn't need to—she was calling for help. He bore down, running as hard as he could. At the same time, Annie slowed to begin her descent into the cave. She called the beast again, and Morgan dove at her, managing to catch her ankle.

Annie went down hard, her face smacking against the stone entrance to the cave. Her call for help stopped abruptly. Morgan held on tight to her ankle, squeezing as hard as he could. He hoped the beast hadn't heard her.

With his hand still wrapped around Annie's ankle, Morgan pushed himself up to his feet and dragged her backward. Annie moaned in obvious pain. She turned back to fight him off. Morgan grimaced when he saw her face. Her mouth dripped blood, one of her teeth had pushed through her upper lip and had been knocked free. The brown tooth hung there, root and all, protruding up through the laceration on her lip. Her jaw hung at an awkward angle. Annie sucked in a long breath to scream again, but only half of her jaw moved while the other half continued to hang there. The impact against the hard stone had broken her jaw in two.

Morgan pulled his eyes away from the bleeding mass of pulp that was the bottom of Annie's face and looked at her eyes. There was a different look there he hadn't seen on her before. Usually, she had a smug look of knowing more than him—about the isle or the beast or eating human meat—but that look was gone. It was replaced with a look of pain and fear.

"Annie, I don't want this for you. I'm sorry you're hurt. Come with me. You will heal. Let me get you out of here," even has he spoke the words, Morgan regretted them. He knew the smart thing to do was to kill Annie and then kill the beast. There was a chance the beast hadn't heard her calls yet. Morgan could still get the drop on the monster, but only if he kept Annie silent. She'd showed him so many times that she didn't want to leave her lover. She wanted to stay. She was his enemy. He should kill her. But still, he couldn't bring himself to do it. If it had been a man, the rock would have already crushed his skull in two places. But Morgan had a soft spot and he knew it.

Annie—through her mangled lips and jaw—managed to let out a scream, but it was garbled with the amount of blood that had filled her mouth. The thick red fluid dripped down her chin and soaked the torn canvas she wore for clothes, but she still screamed. He had to shut her up. Morgan pounced at her.

With all of his weight on her, Annie crumpled down to the ground. Morgan clamped his hand over her mouth to stop her call for help. He held his hand tight over her mouth. He could feel the broken bone of her jaw beneath her papery skin. Blood seeped around his hand and out in-between his fingers. Annie still tried to scream, but the sound was muffled by his hand and garbled from the blood.

"Just be quiet," he said, his face almost touching hers. He realized her mouth was filling with blood and she couldn't breathe when she started coughing and blood flowed from her nose. Her face was beginning to turn purple. He pulled his hand back so she could cough up the blood and clear her airway. He did not want to kill her. Annie's eyes flicked up over Morgan's right shoulder. He didn't have to look to know what was coming. He rolled out of the way just as he heard the loud, unmistakable snarl of the beast. The beast was already in the air when Morgan began his roll and the beast landed, not on Morgan, but instead on Annie. The beast bared its claws and all ten of them plunged into Annie's face and chest. Her body twitched once, blood spurted from every wound, soaking the pale face of the monster. Then Annie's body went limp. Morgan hadn't killed her, but she died anyway.

The beast stared down at his dead lover, in shock, in pain. It was frozen, but only for a moment. The beast freed his claws from the dead woman, turned and looked at Morgan—anger painted across the white face.

Morgan scrambled to his feet. He needed to put some distance between himself and the monster. He'd thought everything through except how to kill the beast. Things were moving fast now, he just had to act.

Without thinking, instead of sprinting away from the beast— who would have been able to catch up to him in only a few strides of his massive legs—Morgan decided to go down inside the cave. The beast might know the cave system better than Morgan, but at least his size would be less of a factor if he had to crouch down. Morgan sprinted down the long access tunnel to the open area. The beast was not far behind him. At least the monster wasn't gaining on him.

When he got inside the large open chamber, Morgan knew the beast would be able to catch up to him. He needed to act quickly once he was there. The faint scent of smoke filled his lungs and it gave Morgan an idea. He put a hand on the wall of the cave, leaned against it for a moment and then propelled himself off the wall and into the open area, giving himself more momentum as the beast would close the gap once it was able to stand up taller. Morgan made for the low burning fire. He skirted around the rocks sticking up from the floor and the snarling beast gained on him. Morgan pulled his foot out of the way just as the beast made a swipe at it with long, bloody claws. The beast wouldn't miss a second time, Morgan needed to move faster.

He bore down, sucking in air and running as hard as he could across the open chamber, but the beast was too fast. Morgan was almost at the fire when he felt a sharp burning pain in his back. He turned and saw the beast just over his shoulder, his mouth wide open revealing multiple rows of small, sharp teeth.

Morgan ignored the claw boring into his back and screamed, throwing an elbow back against the roaring face of the beast and kicking his feet out, anything to get away from the terrible thing. The fire was only a few feet away, he just had to get there before the beast killed him. If he could get to the fire, he still had a chance. A second shot of white-hot pain hit the back of his knee and Morgan screamed even louder, but didn't bother to look back. The beast was toying with him. He could have killed him by now, but was making him suffer instead. Morgan vowed to make the beast pay. Even if he died in the process, he was going to hurt the beast.

He threw an elbow back into the beast's face once more, this one found its mark. Morgan didn't know what he hit, but the beast's hold on him weakened for a moment. It was just enough. He dove at the fire, his hand landing among the hot, burning logs, Morgan didn't care. He wrapped his fingers around one of them. The cave filled with the smell of cooked flesh, but Morgan clung to it instead of letting it go, then he turned and pushed the log into the gaping maw of the beast.

The beast yelped in pain, recoiling as the wood scorched his tongue, gums and lips. Morgan glanced down at his blackened palms, skin hung off them but he ignored the burns and turned back to the fire, he grabbed another, smaller log. Behind him, the beast spit out the first smoldering log and stared at Morgan, wild-eyed.

The beast swiped at him with his deadly claws. The swing was out of control, and Morgan was able to avoid it. His hands still burning and holding onto the hot second log, Morgan charged at the beast and swung the charred, glowing wood at him. Unlike the beast's wild swing, Morgan's attack found its mark and hit the beast square in the chest. The blow wasn't hard enough to do any damage to the massive body of the beast, but the fire on the end of the log did what it was supposed to do. The beast's fur smoldered and smoked moments after Morgan hit him.

The beast staggered again. The air around both of them filled with smoke. Morgan winced, looking down at the mangled mess which had once been the palms of his hands. The smoke got thicker. Morgan watched, waiting for a fire to ignite, but the beast, blinded by the smoke, continued to writhe around swinging its claws at empty space.

In spite of all the smoke, fire was not taking in the beast's fur, as Morgan had hoped. He needed to help it along some more. The remaining logs in the fire were glowing white hot and Morgan could see the flames underneath, ready to burst out as soon as the fire moved around just enough. The pirate-turned-cannibal sucked in a long breath, anticipating the pain that was about to rush through his hands once more. Then he grabbed one of the logs closest to the bottom. He held it at both ends and the heat exploded in his palms once again. Morgan heaved the heavy log at the beast. This time, the log hit the beast on the shoulder. Tiny glowing embers filled the cave. Morgan ducked down and covered his eyes to avoid the hot flakes finding their way inside. The beast's whines and yelps turned into outright screams.

Morgan chanced a look around and popped his head up just long enough to see the embers no longer filled the room. The orange-red embers were gone and smoke had taken their place. Lots of smoke. Then Morgan saw the flames growing on the side of the beast who had taken off and was running further into the darkness of the cave. The flames grew, licking at the air around the beast before he disappeared down into one of the tunnels.

Morgan broke into a series of hard, hacking coughs and only then realized how thick the smoke had gotten. The haze hung from the ceiling and was filling the entire chamber. He knew the beast was headed for the underground spring to douse the flames, but Morgan couldn't follow him or he'd never see the light of day again. He hoped the spring was far enough away that the beast would be burned up long before he got there. If not, there was a good chance the smoke would get the beast instead. Either way, Morgan had to get out.

He stumbled across the open room and managed to find the exit to the cave. By the time he got to the surface, he was hacking and coughing even harder.

Morgan rolled out of the cave and lay on the ground just outside the opening, looking up at the two trees above him. Smoke billowed out of the cave and swirled up into the air. Morgan didn't realize how much smoke had been down there. Was it all from just the burning fur of the beast? He couldn't be sure. He looked over as he lay there, where Annie's body was right next to him. There was a lot of blood, not to mention her mangled face, but she wasn't the first person Morgan had seen run through.

The sun shone down on Morgan, he looked up at it and smiled. He had a nasty cut on his back, a smaller one on his leg that didn't hurt him too much, and his hands were a burnt mess, but he was alive. He had food and water to last him until the *Glory* returned. He had survived the worst Dead Man's Isle had to offer.

16

Morgan's hands throbbed as he lay on the ground. The biggest risk to his life now that Annie and the beast were dispatched with—at least for now—was infection. Aboard the *Glory* his infection risk would be high, given the number of open wounds and sores he had covering his body. Luckily, he was not aboard the ship and he was surrounded by salt water. Morgan was no doctor—no expert—but he knew the salt water would help the healing process and keep his wounds clean. So, Morgan managed to get himself up on his feet, no easy task when he couldn't place either hand down on the ground, but he made it. Then he trekked back across the isle until he got to his beach. He had sprinted to the cave behind Annie, and it felt like it took him no time at all to traverse the distance, but the walk back after his bloody battle with the beast proved to be a lot longer.

At last, he reached his beach. He was the only living thing on Dead Man's Isle and felt secure in that fact. Morgan stripped down, gritted his teeth and entered the ocean. He was fine until the water got to the wound in his back, then the screaming started. Once the cut was complete submerged, Morgan stood with his hands above his head. Slowly he lowered the burnt extremities into the ocean.

The *Glory* was still days away from returning, but every man on the ship could have heard his screams.

Two times a day, every day, Morgan waded up to his neck in the water. His back hurt, but was used to the pain. He had scars on his back from his father before he reached the age of ten. He knew how to deal with that pain. The burns were something different entirely. He'd been burned before. But those burns were nowhere near as severe as his hands. They burned all the time. He didn't sleep well because of the throbbing, itching sensation that coursed from his fingertips all the way up to the middle of his forearm. Even when he plunged them into the ocean water, the feeling was far from refreshing. When they weren't submerged in the painful salt water, his hands were red throbbing pieces of meat with skin and other tissue hanging off them. He didn't have anything clean enough to wrap them in and feared infection, so he kept them out in the air, hoping to dry them out and eventually watch them begin the healing process. Over the course of the next ten days, they did begin to heal. They still hurt and he realized they might never be the same, but his skin was slowly healing, the pain slowly dissipating, though it was never gone completely.

He screamed into the emptiness that surrounded him two times a day, hoping his hands would be healed enough to use when the *Glory* returned. He didn't know what would happen when Captain Avery and the rest of the crew were there. He hoped he could trust Avery, but he still had doubts in the back of his head that the captain would determine his punishment was over.

On the morning of the twelfth day after the death of Annie and the beast, something appeared on the horizon.

Morgan made an effort to scan the horizon on all sides of the isle, knowing eventually the *Glory*—or another ship—would be approaching. When he saw the small dark speck against the clear sky, he didn't get his hopes up that it was the *Glory*, but he prepared himself as though it was. He knew Peter was a person he could trust. His thoughts about Avery changed daily, and this day, he felt as though he could trust the captain as well. Avery assured him his survival on the isle would garner the respect of the other men, but he wasn't sure that was true or not. He'd still killed the first mate, anything was possible. Avery told him he'd need his worst to survive Dead Man's Isle—in that, the captain was correct. But what if he needed his worst to survive aboard the *Glory* once again also? Morgan sat and gingerly picked up a piece of meat, he chewed slowly as he watched the speck grow larger, closer. He had three more pieces of meat and about five more mouthfuls of water. He wouldn't use them all up in case the approaching ship wasn't the *Glory*.

The ship was obviously heading for Dead Man's Isle and, if it wasn't the *Glory*, it looked just like her. In spite of his questions regarding Avery and the crew, Morgan found himself getting excited as the ship grew larger on the calm ocean water. He'd done it, he'd survived Dead Man's Isle.

When the ship was close enough to his beach, Morgan began to wave his arms, shouting up into the air and laughing uncontrollably. He'd done it. Avery had done it, also. But few others had according to the old captain, this was something worth celebrating. Morgan could almost taste the mouthful of rum Avery would give him when the two men celebrated his survival on an island even more inhospitable than he realized when the ship left three weeks earlier.

The ship stopped not far from shore, about the same distance Morgan swam to shore when they first left him there. He was still waving his injured hands and yelling. He could see people on the deck of the ship, though he couldn't make out individual faces, he could tell by the way the man on the bridge of the ship stood and waved, with his left arm tucked tight against his body, that it was Avery. They had come back for him.

17

Morgan barely noticed the pain in his hands as he looked up at the ship that had come back for him until he realized they were dropping anchor. They weren't going to send a raft. If he was going to get off the isle, he was going to have to do it the same way he got there. Stroke after stroke through the salt water and then climb aboard the ship. The thought of it brought a tear to his eyes. Just putting his hands in the water for a few minutes each day was torture, it would take at least ten minutes to swim the distance to the boat. When he got there, he wasn't sure if he'd be able to use his hands to climb back aboard. But he'd made it this far. He'd survived the hunger, the dehydration, the beast, Annie, and the burns. If he could survive all those things, he could survive one final swim. Morgan surveyed his beach. He gingerly scooped up another piece of meat, absently chewed on it and swallowed. He put the bucket to his lips, using his wrists to pick it up and tilt it back. He took two big mouthfuls instead of his usual one. Then he dropped the bucket in the sand and waded out into the water.

He held his arms above his head for as long as he could, stepping through the water as he did so many times before. This time however, he was not returning to the beach. He was going to keep his hands submerged in the water longer than he had ever kept them down before. It was going to hurt, but the end would be worth it.

When the water was above his chest, Morgan stopped. He took a deep breath and looked out at the ship. If he was at his strongest, it would be a five-minute swim, but he was weak, hungry, and injured. It might be ten minutes for him to get there, maybe longer. He'd been counting to a hundred with his hands in the water twice a day and could barely stand it. This was going to be torture—the last test of Dead Man's Isle.

Morgan pressed his lips tight together and plunged his hands down into the water. He didn't scream. Instead, he pushed off the bottom and began to kick. At first, he tried swimming normally, but the movement of his hands through the water made them hurt more, so he kicked hard and moved his hands as little as possible. The pain was still excruciating. His movement forward continued, however. His feet propelled him through the water, his hands he used only to keep himself afloat and steer him in the correct direction. With each kick, his hands throbbed, but the ship got closer. Morgan held his screams in and focused his eyes on the *Glory*, he was halfway there. Three quarters of the way there. Then he was only a few kicks from the ladder on the side of the boat. The men cheered him on when he looked up. The waves crashed into his face and hid the tears of pain and joy washing down his cheeks. He'd done it. He'd survived Dead Man's Isle.

Morgan made the final few kicks and reached up out of the water with a mangled hand, skin hung off it as he raised it up and grabbed onto the first handle of the ladder. He could barely close his fingers around the raised edge, but with a scream of pain, his knuckles closed enough for him to begin his climb.

"Way to go Edward!" The familiar voice of Peter called from above.

"I can't believe it," another, unfamiliar voice said.

A smattering of words came in through his screams. Then the words of encouragement stopped.

"What is that?" someone said.

"It's huge," another person said.

"Swords at the ready," Avery's gruff voice cut through the others.

Morgan didn't have to stop and look over his shoulder to realize what the others were talking about. It was the beast. It had to be.

Morgan picked up his pace. The pain in his hands; gone for now. His only focus was on getting to the deck. The beast was coming for him, but wouldn't care if he took others along with Morgan. If he could just get on deck, the others would be able to fight off the beast.

Morgan grabbed the next rung, and the next. He looked up, only two more to go.

"Hurry up, Mr. Morgan," Avery said. His voice, surprisingly calm, his eyes focused on the water.

The wide-eyed fear on the faces of the men above him was all the encouragement Morgan needed. He hauled himself up the last two rungs all at once. Two men grabbed him and pulled him over the rail onto the deck. He sprawled out, hands numb with pain, but he couldn't just lay there. He pushed himself up to his knees and looked out at the water. The shouts of the men grew louder.

"Where did it go?"

"It's some kind of beast. It will kill us all," Morgan groaned, eyes searching the water for a sign of movement.

He looked down over the rail into the water he'd just been on, straight down the side of the ship. First there was nothing, just the same smooth, blue water he'd seen for almost a month. Then, just below the surface, a flash of white and red, before Morgan could react, the beast broke the surface of the water with a force unlike anything he'd seen before. Water exploded up around the beast as it shot into the air toward Morgan and the crew of the *Glory* behind him.

Gone was the beast's dark fur. Its entire body, except for its paws, looked like Morgan's hands. A mangled pile of healing flesh and meat. The beast grabbed hold of the ladder almost at the top, with one quick pull, it propelled itself up and over the rail and onto the top deck.

Morgan fell flat on his back, watching the beast fly over him. The thing looked even bigger than it had on the isle. As if having something familiar to judge its size made it even more massive.

The beast turned his head, opened his mouth, and snarled when he saw Morgan. It looked toward Avery, stopped and tilted its head to the side, then returned its fuming gaze back to Morgan.

The rest of the men froze in astonishment at the size and appearance of the beast, but Avery's words thawed them.

"Attack the fecker. Get the damned thing off my ship, now!"

That was all it took. The men swarmed it. Morgan looked around and managed to find an extra sword, and he went in on the beast too. At first, it looked like the sheer number of men were going to be too much for the beast. Morgan couldn't see the thing as the men surrounded it. The beast howled as cutlasses poked and prodded at it. But then a few of the men fell back, clutching arms and legs, blood spilling on wood. Then a few more fell away. The beast wasn't just taking hits; it was fighting back.

Morgan moved in close as the beast threw two more men off. Avery continued screaming at the men to attack the thing, so even in the face of fear, they stood up and attacked again with even more vigor. The beast disposed of more men and Morgan saw his opening. The beast's head was turned, looking at one of the others brandishing his own sword. Morgan held his blade tight and instead of swinging it at the beast, decided to take a more direct approach. He held the end of the sword against his chest and ran at the beast, the tip of the blade aimed right for the beast's ribs. Morgan prayed he'd get the sharp point in-between the bones and end the thing once and for all. Morgan screamed as he sprinted toward it. The beast turned at the sound, but it was too late. The tip of the sword made contact right where Morgan planned and the blade kept moving forward. It plunged through the raw pink skin of the beast and buried itself inside.

Initially, nothing changed, the beast still snarled down at

Morgan and began to raise a clawed paw to strike out at him. But Morgan kept pushing. The entire cutlass disappeared inside the beast, leaving only the hilt on the outside of his body. The beast stopped for a moment, so did the rest of the men. Morgan, hands throbbing, barely able to stand, looked up at the beast and smiled. The others began to imitate Morgan's strategy and thrust their blades into the beast as well. Some hit bone, but they pulled the cutlass out and tried again, stabbing and poking holes in the thing over and over repeatedly. Thick, dark, blood coated the deck of the *Glory* and stained the wood. Blood dripped from the beast's mouth. It dropped first to one knee and then flat on its stomach. The men kept up their attack, thrusting swords in and pulling them out again and again. Morgan's cutlass was still buried in the thing and once the beast stopped moving, Morgan built up enough strength to hobble over to the mass of dying meat and withdraw his sword. The beast convulsed a few times on the deck, then became still once again, its blood dripping off the sides of the ship and back into the water. This wasn't the first living thing that had died on the deck, and it wouldn't be the last. It was just another in a long line of deaths the *Glory* had seen in her life.

Morgan held the bloody cutlass up and screamed as he collapsed down on the deck once more. He smiled as the men continued to dissect the body of the dead beast. They sliced off its ears and fingers and then moved on to the bigger pieces of the thing. They laughed and joked as they held up the pieces of its body, then unceremoniously tossed the body parts overboard.

The sword rested against his leg now, and Morgan looked down at the blood dripping off it. Morgan thought about the number of men the beast had eaten in its time on the isle. He raised the sword to his mouth and ran his tongue along the flat part of the sword, tasting the beast as the beast had tasted so many men and women before. The blood tasted sweet and coppery. And good. His mouth full of blood, Morgan dragged himself to his feet once more and spat the red fluid on the beast's mutilated remains.

The men around Morgan erupted in a cheer when he spat. He

held the sword up over his head and screamed, then looked down at the beast in a final act of violence against the already dead beast, Morgan brought the blade down on the beast's neck. It didn't go all the way through, but it made it through to the bone at the back of its neck.

The men surrounded Morgan and kept him from falling back down to the deck once more. He breathed heavily—the enormity of what they'd just done hitting him all at once. The pain in his hand returned almost immediately. Skin and blood and pus dropped off of them, joining the remnants of the beast on deck.

Avery's face appeared in front of Morgan. It was grim, stoic.

"Well done, Mr. Morgan. Let's get you fixed up."

A few men, including Peter and another man Morgan recognized but couldn't recall the name, helped him, not into the bowels of the ship where he normally would have gone to get fixed up, instead they brought him to the Captains Quarter's. Morgan had only been in there once, and it normally wasn't a good thing, he thought this would be a different story.

Before stepping off the main deck, he looked back at the beast as the rest of the men were preparing to push the body overboard and then further out to Dead Man's Isle. He truly had survived, and now it seemed like things were changing.

18

Avery allowed Morgan to do nothing but sleep and eat for a few days after his return to the *Glory*. Morgan didn't realize how hungry and tired he'd been. Once surrounded by the relative safety of the ship, Morgan could feel his body relax, something it hadn't done for almost a month. From the moment he jumped off the side of the ship and swam to the Isle, he'd been in survival mode. The few days of rest let him come out of survival mode and regain some of his strength.

Peter and Avery were his only visitors. Peter, once a day, but Avery shared every meal with Morgan. The two talked about the Isle. Morgan told him everything except about the food he ate. Avery told him he'd never seen the beast, and Morgan judged by the man's age that he was much older than Annie and would not have seen her there either.

Morgan recounted to Avery Annie's account of the pirates that slaughtered and then consumed all the villagers where she had lived with her mother. Avery had not heard the story before, but knew some ships had turned to cannibalism as a way to survive at sea without stopping for supplies for long periods of time.

"In my experience," Avery said. "Something in a person changes once they get a taste for human meat."

Morgan nodded at the comment, but said nothing. He'd told everyone that Annie and the beast had some dried fish on the Isle and he'd eaten their fish once Annie died. Everyone believed it and no one asked any follow-up questions. He had no reason to believe they suspected him of eating human meat the entire time he was there. Plus, they had seen the beast in the water, if the beast wanted to catch fish, he easily could have. Which made Morgan wonder why he didn't. Annie would have died without food. Presumably, the beast would have as well, why then did they wait and risk possible starvation for human meat when the beast could easily have hunted down fish in the water. It didn't make sense to Morgan. The isle, however, was days behind them now, he'd never understand everything that happened there, but it didn't matter. He had survived, that was the only thing anyone cared about.

Most of the crew didn't talk to him, the few comments Morgan happened to catch were whispered complements. Peter told him as much; he'd becoming a legend on the ship. Morgan suspected this might carry beyond the *Glory* and extend to the rest of the seafaring community. His story would become a myth, one passed from sailor to sailor. The Life and Times of Edward Morgan, who survived Dead Man's Isle and its man-eating beast. He smiled to himself; he could learn to live with being a legend.

It sounded like a good thing to be revered by so many of the men aboard the *Glory*, but there was one problem eating away at Morgan. The food he ate; the beans, the dried chicken, even the dried fruit, didn't have enough flavor for Morgan and it didn't fill him up the way it should have—the way it used to. Of course, when he first got aboard, he was starving and ate until he couldn't take another but. Even then, with his stomach full, there was an underlying hunger he could not shake, no matter how much food he ate. Each day that passed, every meal he ate, the hunger grew. It was a different hunger than he felt on the Isle, there, the hunger was caused by a lack of food. This new hunger was caused by a lack of a specific type of food.

Each time Morgan felt the hunger growing inside him, he pushed the feeling away. He explained it to himself as the fact that he was deprived of food for so long, he wasn't sure what it meant to feel full again, and his body was readjusting to having good food inside it again. Once real food worked through his system, feeling the hunger would wane and eventually disappear. Morgan kept waiting, but the hunger, never left him. He needed human meat, and on a ship filled with men, it wasn't going to be hard to find it.

19

On the morning of the day Edward Morgan decided to feed his hunger, the first person he saw was Peter.

Although he'd made the decision to give in to the cravings for human meat, he would not eat Peter, or any of the other men that had been fair to him before he left for Dead Man's Isle. There were enough men he didn't like aboard; he would eat only those men. Morgan had half a sense to let Peter in on his meal decision, but in the end, decided against telling anyone just yet. He hoped he could make a kill, hide the body for a while, and keep everyone guessing as to where his victim ended up. It wasn't unusual for men to fall overboard and never be heard from again. A man could disappear, even on a ship like the *Glory*.

"Morning, Edward." Peter said as the men passed each other on the deck early that morning. Morgan had resumed his normal duties and found he didn't need as much sleep as he used to. He was always at his post early and staying later at the end of his shift. His hands were still a mess—he'd never be able to use them like he did before—but the pain had decreased dramatically and he could do more around the ship each day. Still, there were some tasks—tying knots being the biggest—that he needed help completing.

"Morning, Peter." They stopped and looked out at the glass smooth ocean. The sun was just pushing up on the horizon and the sky was a very light orange hue, it wouldn't be long before the cloudless sky was a light, brilliant blue.

"How're the hands today, any better?"

"They're never going to be normal. I just have to learn how to live with them the way they are. If they keep getting better, then that's a good thing, but if they don't, well, I'll be alright with that, too."

"Did you eat anything today?"

Morgan nodded, stopped himself from smiling at the question. Two men walked by them toward the bow of the ship. They were talking loudly, but the conversation stopped abruptly when they passed Morgan. The entire crew—other than Peter and Captain Avery—were still cautious around him and whispered about him behind his back. He knew the ones who treated him poorly before he left, those were the men he'd eat first. He couldn't wait to taste the tender human meat on his tongue once again.

He spoke with Peter for another few minutes and then each man carried on with his day. Morgan completed the tasks he could, no one complained when he stopped to give his hands a rest for a few moments, even though it was something he'd been reprimanded for in the past. The sun rose and then began its decent.

The day was gone. Morgan's stomach rumbled at the thought of some fresh meat. Once the sun dropped and it was dark out, the hunt would begin.

Activity on the ship slowed down once the sun set. Morgan, still using his private quarters—once reserved for the now deceased First Mate Jarvis—retired for a few hours of rest once it was dark out. Morgan pulled out his knife and checked the sharpness of the blade. He hadn't used it on anything other than rope in a long time, but the blade was still sharp as ever. He ran a whetstone over it a few times just to be sure the blade was ready to slice some meat and take a life.

Morgan watched the moon, when it seemed high enough in

the sky, he made his move. Before leaving his quarters, he lit a candle. It was larger than the usual candles they used aboard the *Glory* and it burned hotter. This would have a specific purpose later, but he was hungry and wanted the flame to be lit when he returned.

Morgan slipped out of his quarters and made his way along the deck looking for someone alone in the dark.

He turned a corner and found the perfect victim. Morgan knew the man only as Nettles and hated him with a passion. Before Morgan's stay on Dead Man's Isle, Nettles was hard on him. He'd been at sea for many years and refused to explain anything to Morgan. He expected Morgan to know everything the first time through, but when Morgan didn't know something, Nettles would ridicule him and encourage the other men to do the same. In a way, Morgan looked at Nettles as the reason he faced so much trouble in his first few months aboard the *Glory*.

Since Morgan's return, Nettles had been nice to him, helping Morgan and explaining things to him he never would have done before. Nettles must have seen the way Morgan and Avery became close and decided it was in his best interest to befriend Morgan, instead of belittle him. Morgan didn't appreciate that, and since he was coming upon Nettles here in the dark, it might be a good time to take out his frustrations on his former tormentor.

"Mr. Morgan," Nettles said, his voice low. All the men, Morgan included, knew better than to wake the captain on a calm night such as this.

"Nettles," Morgan replied. He leaned on the rail of the deck and looked out over the calm ocean around them. The moon shone down and left small ripples of light on the water as it moved. Nettles leaned next to him, as Morgan hoped he would, they watched the water together for a moment in silence before Nettles spoke again.

"Looks like Avery's got you lined up to replace Jarvis as First Mate. Can't say that I blame him. After what you've been through, there isn't nothing that's gonna take you by surprise anymore."

Morgan nodded and let the silence hang between them for a few seconds, then he spoke.

"You know Nettles, there's something I haven't told anyone else about the isle."

"And you're going to tell me now?" Nettles said. He had the smug look on his face Morgan hated. It would make the next few minutes that much more pleasurable.

"I'll have to tell someone, eventually. Might as well be you. The woman I met on the isle and the beast. They were living off dried meat, but it wasn't fish they were living off."

"No," Nettles turned and instead of looking out at the sea, he looked at Morgan. Morgan didn't return the taller man's stare, instead he maintained focus on the water.

"No, I just said that because it was easier than telling the truth. I haven't been on the water long and had never heard of Dead Man's Isle until Avery told me about it. I didn't know most pirates look at it as a place to leave men and have a guarantee they won't survive. Most captains don't come back to check on their men. Not sure why Avery decided to check on me this time, but I'm glad he did. Point is, men have been getting dropped off at the isle for years and left for dead. The woman and her beast weren't eating fish they caught and dried, I know because I tried to catch fish in the water around there and there were none. Even if there were fish, they wouldn't have wanted it, because they'd gotten a taste for human meat."

He felt Nettles' eyes on him but continued to watch the sea.

"The thing is, if I was going to survive, it seemed like I might have to eat it, too. It was the meat of all the men that had been left on the Isle over the years. The beast catches them, kills them, and they have a salt deposit or something in a cave under the isle. They dry out the meat and salt it and then eat it. One person after another. The reason I was able to survive? Because they'd just had a man left there not too long before me. They decided to keep me alive while they ate the other guy first."

'Why are you telling me this, Morgan? What did you eat?"

"Annie—the woman there—she kept telling me that when you get a taste for human meat, it changes you." Morgan closed his hand around the handle of the knife under his shirt.

"What are you saying Morgan? Shite, out with it."

"I would have died if I didn't eat it, Nettles. But she was right, it did change me," Morgan moved fast. Before Nettles could react, he pulled the knife out and plunged it into his throat. Nettles made a quick gagging sound before the blade completely punctured his windpipe and no sound could escape his mouth. Morgan grabbed the back of Nettles' head and pushed the man against the knife, making sure he cut through as much of his neck as possible. The warm blood gushed around his hand and down his arm. The smell of blood and fresh meat made Morgan's mouth water.

The original plan was to keep the body and eat it slowly over the course of a few days and hope he wasn't found. But Morgan thought it might be easier to get rid of the body immediately after harvesting what he needed from Nettles. He withdrew his knife. Nettles was still looking at him, blinking and feebly trying to stop the blood from gushing out of his throat. It didn't matter if Nettles was alive or dead. The only sound Nettles made was a low, gurgling sound as air was leaving his lungs, causing the blood on his neck to bubble up. No one would hear that. So, Morgan lay Nettles down and began to carve him up.

All of the meat wouldn't keep and Morgan couldn't eat everything that night so he only butchered what he could eat in the next day or two. Everything else he would have to toss overboard. Eventually, he'd have to do it to someone else though. He might be able to go a few weeks before he needed to feed on a human again. Once he finished this meal, the hunger would remain in check. He'd be able to have some form of self-control, at least for the short-term.

Morgan decided to use the legs, because they have the most muscle and were probably the easiest to carve up. Morgan made a long slice down one side of Nettles' calf. Nettles made a few involuntary movements, and then stopped moving. Morgan made a similar cut along the other side of the calf and a long thin piece of meat came right off. He laid it down on the deck and moved to the other calf. Repeating the process, he ended up with two identical strips of meat.

Next, Morgan ripped off Nettles' clothes so he could get at his thighs and rump. He carved the thighs up in a similar fashion as the calves and lay the meat on the deck. A few times he heard noises, but they were tucked away on the far corner of the ship and there would need to be a reason for someone to come over and check out what was happening. It was a clear night, nothing was happening, no one would check. After cleaning the thighs almost to the bone, Morgan realized he probably had more than enough meat to last him until it started to go bad. He wasn't going to eat rotten meat, so the best course of action was to stop.

He tucked the knife away in his blood-soaked shirt once again and knelt down. With so much meat missing from his body, Nettles was surprisingly easy to pick up. Morgan dragged him over to the rail and dropped him unceremoniously into the water, hoping the current would carry him away, or a shark would get a whiff of blood in the water and look for a quick meal.

With the remains taken care of, Morgan picked up two of the slippery pieces of meat and brought them back to his quarters, then he returned, took the second two pieces, and brought them back as well. His clothes were stained crimson, front and back, and there was a trail of blood leading to his door, but Morgan didn't care at the moment. He needed to eat.

He cut a few small pieces off the thigh and skewered them on the end of his knife. Then he held the meat over the flame he lit before he left. He could still see the hairs on the skin as he touched the meat to the flame, but they quickly burned up. His quarters filled with the beautiful odor of freshly cooked meat. When the pieces of Nettles appeared to be cooked enough on the outside, Morgan pulled them off of the flame. He blew on the meat once, twice and then a third time. He didn't want to burn his mouth because then the meat wouldn't taste as good. When he figured it was cool enough, he used the knife as a fork and plucked the first piece off with his lips.

Morgan moaned as he chewed, the human meat filling his mouth, the delicate flavor danced on his tongue. It was perfection. Dried human meat was alright, but not that much different in texture from every other dried meat he'd eaten. Cooked human meat was exquisite. The smooth buttery flavor of Nettles' thigh filled his mouth and danced on his tongue. He ate the second piece in the same, slow deliberate manner. He didn't just eat it, he experienced it, and savored each morsel. This was what he'd been dreaming of.

20

Morgan woke to a pounding at the door to his quarters. He was still wearing the bloody clothes from the night before. The pieces of Nettles he hadn't eaten were laying in the middle of the floor, the candle still burning, though it was lower than the last time he'd seen it. He must have passed out shortly after ingesting the wonderful human meal.

"Mr. Morgan," Avery's voice called from the other side of the door.

"Shite," Morgan cursed under his breath. He'd not cleaned up the trail of blood. When someone noticed Nettles was missing, Morgan would immediately become the number one suspect. He sprang up and ripped off the dirty clothes, using them to wipe the dried blood off his hands and face as best he could. "One moment, Captain."

Morgan found a shirt and pants that weren't covered in blood and managed to throw them on. He grabbed the knife, too, and slid it inside his shirt. He didn't want to kill the captain, but he would if he had to.

He pulled the door open just enough so he could slide out of the room and pulled the door shut behind him. Avery was standing there and did not look happy.

"Captain," Morgan said, hoping there wasn't a massive amount of blood on his face.

"Morgan, I think you have a problem here," Avery looked down and then along the wood of the deck, there was more blood than Morgan realized. It had been too dark to see much the night before.

"I—yes. I can see that. I just..." Morgan stammered and then trailed off. He held the knife tight in his hand ready to drive it into Avery's throat, depending on the next words that came out of his mouth.

"Tell me what happened, Morgan. I'm glad you survived that isle, but it's still my ship. If you didn't learn nothing from the isle, maybe I should bring you back."

"Yes, I understand that. I'm not sure you would believe me if I told you. I'll try to explain."

"I want to hear all of it, Morgan. Not bollocks from you."

"No. Of course."

"My quarters. Yours looks like it might need some cleaning."

Morgan followed Avery around to the opposite side of the ship where the captain's quarters were. They were directly opposite from the first mate's quarters, but were larger. Morgan had been in the captain's quarters quite a bit lately and the fact that he was going there was not out of the ordinary, so no one took notice of them.

Morgan followed Avery inside and pulled the door shut. It squeaked as he pulled it closed. Avery sat down behind his small desk.

"Talk."

"I didn't mean for it to happen."

"Nettles?"

"Yes."

"You killed him?"

"Yes, but that's only part of it." Morgan took a deep breath and fingered the knife yet again. "I didn't eat fish on the isle."

"I know, Morgan. I survived there too, remember," a slight smile crept across Avery's lips. "I told you, eating human meat does something to us. It changes us. The beast sure knows how to kill humans when it wants to."

"The beast was there when you were there?"

"Aye. Like you, it had recently had another kill. It wanted to keep me alive and fresh. I befriended it. We ate the person that had come before me. I helped it kill a person while I was there and then I left —the beast let me leave—on the next ship."

"You didn't tell me."

"This isn't a charity, Mr. Morgan. You were sentenced to death. I thought you might be able to survive. I didn't think it would be the way that it happened. That beast has killed more people than either of us can imagine. I got the hunger too, like you did. I took command of another ship—violently. It was a mutiny. But the men —the men loved me. So, they followed me. I met a woman, had a child and took them to an island not far from here. I left them in a village because the hunger was too great, a pirate ship is no place for women and children anyway. Then one day, I lost it. I returned to that village and slaughtered them all. I ate the villagers and my men joined me. We ate them all. I had created a whole ship of monsters who were hungry for human meat. I tried to control them, but I couldn't. The only person I could save was my daughter. I couldn't keep her safe. Not even from m'self. Not on that ship. So, I brought her to the isle and convinced my beast-friend to keep her alive for me." Avery stopped and made the same gagging sound Annie had made on the isle. The beast's name. Now, because of Morgan, the beast and Annie were both dead. Avery's friend and his...daughter?

"Annie was your daughter? I tried to get her to come with me."

"Aye. I don't blame you for her death, Morgan. She had lived off human meat for over twenty years. She's more of a monster than you or I by this point. I'm sure you did the best you could. The beast didn't even recognize me when he was on the ship. Maybe he wasn't such a friend after all." Avery reached down behind the small desk and produced a jug and two glasses. The crew was only allowed rum on special occasions, but the captain had his own supply and could partake any time he wished. Avery set both glasses down on the table and filled them from the bottle. The captain raised his glass and Morgan followed suit. Morgan let Avery drink first, they both took a mouthful, Avery put his half-full glass back down on the table, Morgan held his.

"So, you killed and ate Mr. Nettles last night then. Am I right?"

Morgan nodded.

"I understand. The urge is hard to control. I wish you'd told me sooner. I could have helped you get control of the thing. It's hard. Taken my years to learn how to control it. Now, I wait until I can do things properly. I don't let the hunger control me, Mr. Morgan. You can do that, too. I know you can."

"That was my plan. But I needed something to tide me over. I figured it would be a few weeks—maybe a month—before I got the urge again after last night. No one likes Nettles anyway."

"It's not the point, Mr. Morgan. You've got to control it all the time. Of course, I want to eat you. I want to eat every man on this ship. But I can't. I have to pick who I slaughter. Then when I get the chance. I do it slowly. I enjoy it. I don't cook small pieces of them over a candle flame. I roast large cuts of them over a fire, on a spit, and then gorge myself, because if I'm going to do it, I might as well enjoy every second of it."

"I couldn't stop myself. I am sorry, Captain Avery."

"Ah, don't say sorry. You and me are a type of monster no one will ever understand, Mr. Morgan. They can't unless they've done what we've done, seen what we've seen and ingested what we've ingested. Keep me informed next time. And don't kill anyone on this ship. I will deflect suspicion from you, the men still revere you— that will last—so it shouldn't be too hard. I will get us to port soon and then you can feed. Or work on your will power until we can do things the proper way. Choke down the food we have on board to stay alive and then wait for our feast."

"I will Captain. Thank you," Morgan raised his glass and gulped down the rest of the rum, then left Avery's quarters and returned to his own.

21

Morgan managed to not kill anyone else. He cooked a few more pieces of Nettles and threw the meat overboard once it went bad. The *Glory* made it to port inside of three weeks and though the hunger was still there—it would always be there, Morgan knew now —he held it at bay. When the ship docked, Morgan was the first off the ship. He began hunting for a meal almost immediately.

The village they'd docked at was not the largest Morgan had ever been to, but it wasn't small either. There were families and sturdy buildings set up in the settlement. As he travelled further away from the dock and the main business area of the village, the number of buildings dwindled quickly as did the quality of their construction. There were less crowds also, which meant it would be easier for Morgan to find someone on their own. One person missing from the village would hardly be noticed.

Avery tried to convince Morgan to wait a little longer and do things right, but Morgan couldn't hold the hunger at bay. He needed to eat. He moved like a panther in the jungle, hiding in the shadows, waiting for someone to come along, alone.

There was a large boulder along one of the main paths leading into the village. He ducked behind it, held his freshly sharpened knife to his chest and waited. Most people travelled in pairs, but some travelled alone. Morgan waited for a weak one to come along. Finally, a woman came, Morgan had seen her in the village earlier with a man, now she was alone. It was perfect.

He crouched low behind the rock and waited until the woman strolled past. When she was on the other side, he snuck out from behind the boulder and took a few quick steps up behind her. He didn't wait to stop her and talk like he had with Nettles. He didn't mirror her movements like he'd done with Annie on Dead Man's Isle. This wasn't about a confession or about trying to save her, this was only about the hunt, the kill, the meal. He held the knife tight in his right hand, preparing to drive the point into her side between the rib, yank it out quick then slice her throat. Just as Morgan pulled the knife back for his first thrust, a heavy blow hit him on the side of the head. He groaned and crumpled to the ground.

Morgan was dazed, but only for a second. He blinked twice and saw a figure above him. It was the man he'd seen with the woman at the settlement. He'd been blinded by his hunger and had not checked to make sure the woman was alone. Luckily, Morgan still held on to the knife, and when the man came down on him, yelling at him in Spanish, Morgan thrust the knife upward into his gut.

The man grunted, and the knife slid into him, but not very far, and the pain had little effect on him. While Morgan was looking down at the man's stomach and his failed knife attack, he was hit again by something heavy on the side of the head. The impact turned his face and he fell again to the ground. It was the man's fist. After the second blow, the knife fell from Morgan's grip and lay on the dirt. Morgan scrambled to get back to his feet, but the hits to his skull disoriented him. Before Morgan could get up and dive for the knife, the man was on top of him, screaming this time as he rained punches and forearms down on Morgan's back. Luckily, none of the strikes were hard and Morgan had worked himself almost back to his feet. But before he could get to the knife, an arm wrapped itself around Morgan's neck and squeezed. Morgan tried to suck in a breath, but couldn't.

Morgan's hands instinctively went to his throat, he pulled at the man's arm, but couldn't break the chokehold. His head felt like it was going to pop. He needed to get out of the man's grasp. Morgan stopped struggling. It wasn't going to get him free, he needed to change his tactic. He stood still and limp, even as he felt himself struggle for air, he wanted the man—who had probably never killed another man—to believe he'd passed out or died. The man relaxed his hold a slight amount and it was all Morgan needed.

Morgan turned his head just enough and opened his mouth, a small part of the man's arm pushed its way inside his mouth. Morgan bit down as hard as he could. Not like a man fighting another man, but as a hungry cannibal looking for his next meal. He tore at the man's flesh, his mouth filled with warm delicious blood. The man's grip on his throat released. He should have used that reprieve to suck in as much air as he could muster, but instead he just bit down harder. The man howled in pain and tried to shake Morgan free, but it only made Morgan squeeze down on his arm harder.

The man bucked and swung his arm back and forth so hard, Morgan was able to pull a chunk of meat from his arm. Morgan fell one way and the man in the opposite direction, they both collapsed down on the ground. There was screaming in the distance, but Morgan barely heard it. He had a mouth full of meat and he stared at the man clutching his bloody arm.

Eating raw meat was different. It didn't taste as good, but the experience was something different entirely. Seeing the man clutching his arm, seeing the expression on his face as Morgan chewed on his flesh brought the act of cannibalism to a different level. The muscle and sinew was chewy, and some pieces stuck between his teeth as he savored every moment. Once he had worked it into a soft enough pulp, he swallowed the warm, uncooked meat down.

The man—and the woman who had since joined him—stared at him in horror. Morgan grinned at them, teeth and lips covered in bright red blood.

Movement behind him caught his attention and he turned as men from the village swarmed him and wrestled him to the ground. The newcomers and the man spoke in Spanish to each other, and then the group of newcomers also stared at Morgan, obviously unbelieving what they just heard. Morgan smiled at them as he had the man whose flesh sat digesting in his stomach. Avery—he hoped —would get him out of this.

They tied him up, put chains around his wrists, then carried him back to the village.

22

The jail was just one small room with walls on three sides and wooden bars that acted as a door. If Morgan had his knife with him, he'd be able to cut through the wood and get out on his own. He didn't, though. Still, it wasn't like he'd killed anyone. He'd wanted to, but in the end, he'd just had a little taste of what he wanted. Avery would get him out, if not today, then he'd just sit in the jail until the *Glory* left port, at which time Morgan would go with them. There wouldn't be any sort of punishment from the villagers. None from Avery as well. Avery understood what Morgan was going through. Morgan had survived Dead Man's Isle. No one could touch him now, not even the infamous Captain Avery.

A guard sat nearby, though he barely looked into Morgan's small cell. When he did, Morgan grinned at him, wondering if his teeth were still stained red.

He kept waiting for Avery, Peter, or one of the other men from the *Glory* to come and see him. But none of them did. The sun rose and set and Morgan slept the night in the cell, hoping the morning would change his situation.

When morning came, there was still no sign of Avery. Eating a single bite of the man the day before had done nothing but strengthen the hunger. He needed to eat. Chicken or pork or rice or beans were not going to cut it. He needed human meat. The guard changed a few times over the course of the day and night, but each one looked more delicious than the last.

Finally, Morgan heard a familiar voice from somewhere outside the cell that he couldn't see. He stood, brushed himself off, and waited for Avery to come into view. When the captain came around the corner, he wasn't alone.

"Mr. Morgan, you're in a lot of trouble. You understand that?"

Morgan nodded.

Avery had brought three other men with him; Peter was among them. Morgan made eye contact with his friend and gave him a short nod. Peter stared back; his face unfriendly. Avery took a step forward, his face against the wooden bars. He lowered his voice so only Morgan could hear.

"The reason I get to eat what I eat is because I don't call attention to it. You keep doing these things and I won't protect you. Hard to protect you right now. You're bringing too much attention to it. You have to learn, sometime."

Morgan still said nothing, nodded and looked back at the captain. It was in that moment Morgan realized Captain Avery had to die. Avery stepped away and spoke loud enough for everyone to hear again.

"They are keeping you in here until tonight. I'll be back to take you sometime after dark. We'll go right to the ship and you'll stay on her until morning when we shove off. Any problems between now and when we leave, I'll leave you here with them. Do ye understand?"

Again, Morgan said nothing, he simply nodded again and thought of ways to kill Captain Avery.

Morgan refused food the rest of the day and the hunger inside him grew with each passing second. He dreamed of killing Avery with his teeth, just clamping his jaws around the man's neck and tearing him apart until he lay a mutilated mess on the ground, blood and pulp and bone barely recognizable as a human. But Avery was too smart to let that happen. Even if Morgan took him by surprise, he'd survive the initial attack and would have a weapon on him or nearby, and that would be the end of Edward Morgan. There was so much more Morgan wanted to do with his life. He'd waited too long to taste the pleasures of human flesh and he needed to experience it all before he died. The meat of a woman, for instance, was something he was so close to tasting only a few days before, and that was now still a dream. He wanted to relive the feeling of eating a person while they were still alive, watching him swallow them and ingest them. He wanted to roast a whole person over a fire like a pig. So much still needed to be done, and Avery was trying to put a stop to that. And why? To make things easier for himself. If Avery was an obstacle, Avery had to die. Maybe Morgan would roast Avery over an open fire.

Darkness came and the guard switched once more. Morgan stood and waited. He didn't have a plan, but would be ready in case an opportunity arose to take Avery by force. If Avery came alone, he might even try jumping on and pounding the older man into submission.

The night stretched on. The anticipation Morgan felt when the sun first set was gone. He hadn't eaten a thing in two days except for the single bite of the villager's arm, and he wanted more. Now he didn't even care if it was human meat or not, he needed something to relieve the knot in his stomach. Even the guard fell asleep and was snoring out in front of the cell and still, Morgan waited. He wondered for a brief moment if Avery and the *Glory* had just left him there, determined to let the villagers do what they wanted with him. Maybe Avery could read his mind and knew what he was planning. Rather than deal with Morgan, Avery just decided to let him rot there. But Avery did come, and he came alone.

"Knew you'd be awake, Mr. Morgan," Avery said when he appeared as if from thin air on the other side of the wooden bars. He tapped the bars gently with his fingers as he stood there. "I waited until the guard here and most everyone else was asleep."

"You gonna get me out of here or leave me?"

"I told you what was going to happen. I always know how things will happen. You an' me, we're like brothers now. Family. We have to look out for each other."

"Like you looked out for Annie?" Morgan knew the comment would hit Avery hard. Maybe he should have waited for the old man to take him out of the cell before he made a comment like that. Too late though.

Avery's face darkened; his eyes narrowed.

"I do somethin' to you Mr. Morgan? I told you to wait and not make a mess in this village. You're the one who can't listen to nothing other than the hunger. I see it in your eyes. You can't take it much longer. That ain't you talking just now. It's the hunger. You probably having some thoughts, too. About breaking out, killing the whole village. Eating them. Maybe even killing me. It's hard to stop those things once the hunger gets a hold of your thoughts. You gotta fight back against those thoughts, hear me?"

"I do, I'm trying." Morgan said. He realized Avery was right, but even as he spoke the words, he could picture himself turning Avery's body on a spit.

"That's all I ask. We will get the hunger under control Mr. Morgan. But you have to listen to me, aye."

"Aye," Morgan replied. Avery went to the guard and carefully removed the key from the sleeping man's hand. "No need to make a big thing of it."

Avery opened the door and led Morgan out into the night. They walked slowly, but with purpose, through the jungle surrounding the outskirts of the village. Morgan could see lights from the village through the trees in front of them and beyond that, a few lights from the deck of the *Glory*. As he'd suspected, Avery got him out of the village jail without any further punishment.

He could grab Avery at any moment and be done with him. Avery led the way and was a slight bit shorter than Morgan, all he had to do was come up behind him and wrap an arm around his throat. He'd squeeze so hard the captain wouldn't have a chance to turn on him—or bite off a chunk of flesh—Morgan would squeeze until his head popped off. But Avery told him to not let the hunger take control of him. Morgan didn't want to seem weak, so he let things be.

"This way," Avery's gruff voice cut through the night. He led them down an embankment and through some thick trees, then Avery stopped and held up his hand. Morgan tried to look past him, but couldn't see anything other than the dark leaves.

"What is it," Morgan whispered.

"Here, take this," Avery turned.

In the dark, Morgan couldn't see what Avery was giving him so he felt around with both hands. He felt something on one wrist then the other. Before Morgan could react, the rope had been pulled tight and his wrists were caught.

"What is this?" Morgan yelled into the darkness. He tried to pull his hands apart but somehow, Avery had gotten both hands looped and tied together without him realizing it.

Morgan took a step back and another rope pulled tight around his ankle. Fire lit up around him. They were in a small clearing; Avery had lit a few torches. Morgan struggled but was caught.

"I told you to work on those knots, Mr. Morgan. Knots are the most important thing at sea, remember me telling you that?"

"What do you want?" Morgan struggled again, but with one foot on the ground and the other being pulled toward one of the trees, he lost his balance and—unable to brace himself—

fell down on his face.

Avery laughed. It reminded Morgan of Annie's laugh; his heart sank. He had an idea of what Avery had in mind.

"I'm not the only pirate to drop men off at Dead Man's Isle. Not by a long shot. But I must drop off more than most. I didn't want my daughter to starve. Had to help her out somehow, you understand. How was she? She was alright? No, no don't tell me. I imagine her living there, the beast protecting her and keeping her safe, then killing the men for her so they could both eat and stay alive." Avery moved about the clearing as he spoke. Morgan kept trying to get out of the ropes, but each attempt proved more futile than the last.

"You think you're the only one with the hunger inside you, Mr. Morgan. We might have survived the Isle, but we're far from the same. You can have the ability survive, but you have to have the will power to control the hunger, too. You had the ability, but you seem to be lacking in the willpower. I can't keep you on my ship, Mr. Morgan. You'll eat the whole crew, eventually. When I heard you ate the chunk of that man while he watched, I knew there was no hope for you. Seeing someone watch while you ingest them, it's almost too much to take. The hunger gets almost too strong that way. I was like you once. I ate a man piece by piece while he watched and it turned me into a monster. For three years I couldn't be around anyone else. I couldn't control myself. Then one day something changed inside me. I built up the will power and was able to stop myself."

Avery stepped back into the light. He held a torch and threw it on a pile of dried wood at the center of the clearing. The flames grew quickly. He knelt next to the fire and rose up; he held a knife in one hand and a rope in the other.

"But from time to time, I just let the hunger take over and do what it wants to do," Avery stalked toward Morgan.

"Please. You don't have to do this Avery. I will be safe. I'll have the willpower. I'll control the hunger."

"I know I don't have to do this. I *want* to do this. The hunger has been telling me to do this for months. I've controlled myself for a long time, but I'm not controlling it anymore."

Avery came at him and was on him before Morgan even realized it. He never touched the ropes on his hands, but even as Morgan kicked his one free leg, Avery managed to get a rope around both ankles. Then he cinched both ropes tight. Morgan could struggle, but he couldn't move very far and he couldn't break free. With a few grunts and moving around, Avery was able to hoist Morgan up. He hung upside down from one of the trees, his head just a meter off the ground.

"What are you going to do?" Morgan asked, feeling resigned to the fact that he would probably die here unless someone came to save him. No one on the ship was going to stand up to Avery. This looked like it was the end of the line for him.

"Mr. Morgan, you should know what I'm going to do. I'm going to make you watch me eat you. And then I'm going to leave you here to bleed out and die."

Avery took the knife to Morgan's clothes, cutting them off his body until there was enough of him exposed that the old cannibal could carve any piece of Morgan he wanted from his body with ease.

"My favorite are the thigh muscles," Avery said. There was no anger in his voice. Instead, he sounded calm, content, and happy. "I always start there first."

Morgan prepared himself for the pain and screamed into the night when Avery pushed the sharp knife into his upper thigh. Blood dripped down his body and into his face as the cutting continued. His entire leg throbbed, so he didn't know exactly when the cutting was done. When he managed to control his screaming, he opened his eyes. Avery stood in front of him, a large piece of dripping flesh in his hand.

Avery placed Morgan's thigh muscle on the ground and cut it into small cubes.

"It cooks faster this way," Avery said as he slid the cubes of meat onto a long sharp stick. Morgan's breathing quickened. Blood and sweat dripped down his face and onto the grass just below him. Avery walked over to the fire which Morgan could see if he strained his neck far enough to one side. He held the meat into the flames for a minute or two. The air filled with the scent of cooked flesh. Morgan's mouth watered. The hunger was begging him for a bite even though he knew it was his own.

Avery returned with a smile on his face. He knelt down and held Morgan's cooked flesh in his face.

"Smell it?" Avery said.

Morgan looked up at him. His leg throbbed harder. He felt dizzy and wondered how much longer it would be before he passed out.

"Smell's good doesn't it, Mr. Morgan?"

Morgan nodded. Avery laughed.

"The hunger has you in its grip so tight right now, Mr. Morgan. You want a bite don't you."

Morgan said nothing.

Avery pulled a cube of meat from the stick with his fingers and popped it into his mouth. He chewed, closed his eyes and moaned in pleasure.

"You taste delicious, Mr. Morgan. Would you like a bite?"

Morgan still didn't say anything, didn't move. But when Avery brought a cube of meat to his mouth, Morgan opened his mouth. Avery pushed the piece of Morgan in and Morgan closed his lips around his own thigh, along with the tip of Avery's finger. He chewed. The feeling was amazing.

Avery laughed into the night and finished off the rest of the meat on the skewer.

With the skewer empty, he went to work on Morgan's other thigh. He screamed again as more pain ripped through his body and blood dripped onto his face. Then his eyes began to close. The pain was too much. He felt tired, weak. He couldn't take anymore.

"Please, please," Morgan begged, but he wasn't sure if the words were coming out of his mouth or just in his head. Avery held a piece of meat in front of his mouth again. Morgan parted his lips for one more taste, but before the warm flesh touched his lips, the world went black.

THE END

AFTERWORD

I almost always spend a lot of time brainstorming before I start writing because it helps me get inside the characters heads. With the book you're holding now, I didn't do that right away. I started with the first scene then figured out the plot of the rest of the book after that scene was written.

Writing a book is a solitary activity but it takes a lot of people working together to publish one. A million thanks to everyone who helped make this book possible. Thanks first to my publishers Dawn and Tim who are always helpful and supportive. Thanks to Ash Ericmore for creating such an awesome cover. Thanks also to Tasha Schiedel for editing and finding all the mistakes I made along the way. Thanks to Candace Nola, and Steve Stred for reading this early and providing some great blurbs for the book. As always thanks to Mandy, Tom and Isabella for putting up with me and letting me get into the writing zone one or two times a day. I couldn't have done this without them. Finally, and most importantly, thanks to you for buying a copy of this book and reading it. Every page you read, review you leave, and friend you tell about my books, means more than you know.

Now, batten down the hatches, me hearties, and join me in the briny deep.

Joe Scipione
April 2023

JOE SCIPIONE

Joe Scipione is the author of *Mr. Nightmare, Zoo: Eight Tales of Animal Horror, Decay* and *Perhaps She Will Die*. He lives in the suburbs of Chicago with his wife and two kids. He is a member of the Horror Writer's Association and a Senior Contributor and horror book reviewer at Horrorbound.net. When he's not reading or writing you can usually find him cheering on one of the Boston sports teams or walking with his dog around the lakes near his home. Find him on twitter: @joescipione0 or at www.joescipione.com

ABOUT THE EDITOR / PUBLISHER

Dawn Shea is an author and half of the publishing team over at D&T Publishing. She lives with her family in Mississippi. Always an avid horror lover, she has moved forward with her dreams of writing and publishing those things she loves so much.

D&T Previously published material:
    ABC's of Terror
    After the Kool-Aid is Gone

Follow her author page on Amazon for all publications she is featured in.
    Follow D&T Publishing at the following locations:
    Website
    Facebook: Page / Group
    Or email us here: dandtpublishing20@gmail.com

The Life and Times of Edward Morgan by Joe Scipione

Edited by Tasha Schiedel

Cover by Ash Ericmore

Formatting by J.Z. Foster

The Life and Times of Edward Morgan

www.ingramcontent.com/pod-product-compliance
Lightning Source LLC
Chambersburg PA
CBHW052007220626
47052CB00004B/1126

* 9 7 8 1 9 5 9 7 7 8 3 9 4 *